Moonlit Road

Pearl Lake, the Moonlit Trilogy
Book Three

Tina Marie

This is a work of fiction. Names, characters, businesses, places, events, and incidents are either the products of the author's imagination or used in a fictitious manner. Any other resemblance to actual persons, living or dead, or actual events is entirely coincidental.

Pearl Lake, The Moonlit Trilogy Book 3 Moonlit Road

Copyright © 2019 Tina Marie

Cover Image provided by Bob and Val West

All rights reserved. No part of this book shall be uploaded, reproduced, transmitted or distributed in digital, or paper reproduction without the written consent of the author. If you're wishing to use any part of this book for reviews or articles, please use it in quotations. Thank you for understanding the author's rights.

ISBN: 9798646885198

Acknowledgments

Janine Bernaldez thank you for your eagle eyes and everything else, there is too much to even begin to mention. I appreciate all your help and yes, your friendship too. To Bob and Val West, I love both of your skills. Behind the lens and Val your photo editing skills are amazing! Thank you both for allowing me to showcase your work. To both my sisters, thank you. I won't go into to details but you both know why. And to my husband. Again. Thank you for putting up with me bouncing words off you and also understanding that when I tell you to shush, you don't take it to heart, but know it's only because I'm thinking. Marie Saunders, thank you for your help in getting it right. To all my readers. I can't express how happy I am that you have come to love the Pearl Lake Trilogy. If I continue writing, that Trilogy will have birthed a series. For each and everyone of you for taking the time to message me or leave a review online is so very appreciated and I thank you! After all, if it wasn't for the readers, why write…~ Tina

Dedication

To my kids. Know that you two are the most important people to have entered my life and I'll love you forever.

Part One

Chapter 1

"Abbi! For God's sake, slow the hell down!" Kim yelled from the back seat for the tenth time.

Abbi was zoned out. And just like the last time Kim went on a tirade, she was ignored. If anything, it made Abbi want to go faster. Zipping past the cars and transports, her only thought was that she needed to get to Ben, and now.

The plan had been to fly. Nigel, her real estate agent had 'connections' and assured her that he could find her a jet; and he did, but not for at least a week. God Himself couldn't keep her waiting for a week. They had to leave now, and their only option was to drive.

Abbi hated travelling on the 401, almost as much as she hated flying. But nothing was going to stop her, not even her fear. She gripped the steering wheel a little tighter as she read the sign on the side of the road... London, population 353 000, 4 interchanges.

Great. Just what I need. Traffic is going to pick up again...

"Mom?" Ava's soft voice broke into her musings.

"Yeah?" Abbi responded, never taking her eyes off the road.

Ava knew that look on her mother's face and it wasn't good. They had been on the road for 5 hours. Traffic had been brutal through Toronto. But that hadn't stopped her mother from keeping the speed at a constant 130 km. She had to be getting tired.

"Why don't we stop for a minute? There is a service station just past London. We can grab a bite to eat and a coffee." Ava suggested.

"Yeah, and I really need to take a piss." Kim chimed in from the back seat, groaning her need.

Abbi adjusted the rear-view mirror until she caught Kim's image in the reflection. She *was* squirming an awful lot.

"Fine. Five minutes and we're back on the road," Abbi agreed. She hated the thought of even stopping for five minutes. That was five minutes too long. But she had to admit she needed to make a stop to the ladies' room herself. It was starting to get dark. The city lights of London were now behind them as Abbi stepped on the gas pedal. The sooner they got there, the sooner they could leave.

Ava and Kim grabbed the 'oh shit' bars as the SUV swerved around a transport. Flying past it, they all failed to see the OPP cruiser right in front of it.

"Son of a bitch!" Abbi swore, as the cruiser's lights engaged.

The signs for the service station were right there… just 5 more kilometers. She had to stop. And she would… at the service station. Never batting an eye, Abbi kept her speed steady. Mentally she counted down each kilometer.

"Uh… Abbi? You gonna stop or what?" Kim asked. Abbi flipped her lid; Kim just knew it.

"Mom? Pull over before you get yourself arrested," Ava reasoned.

Not trusting her sister to stop, Kim leaned between the seats and pointed, "There's the merge lane for the service station. Get the hell over Abbi."

Abbi quickly clicked on her signal. Slowing down, she exited the highway and came to a stop in an open area of the parking lot.

"Jesus, Abbi what the hell were you thinking?" Kim questioned, shaking her head.

With a heavy sigh, Abbi rummaged in the center console for her ownership and insurance.

"I'm not... thinking that is." She shot a quick glance to her two companions. "If I don't get arrested. One of you will need to drive. I um... I need a break." She whispered, her voice cracking at her admission.

"Sure, honey." Kim's voice softened. "One of us will drive, won't we Ava?"

"Yeah mom, we can take turns." Ava reached over, giving her mom a hug.

A knock at Abbi's window had them all jumping. Turning to look out the glass, Abbi saw the police officer standing there. She hit the power window button. As it lowered, she glanced up at the angry face peering down at her.

"Ma'am... license and registration, please."

Without a word, Abbi handed over the requested documents.

"You do realize you were going 140, right? I could haul you in for stunt driving and impound your car. Mind telling me what's so important that you're willing to risk the lives of others on the road and your passengers?" the officer asked, bending down to look at Ava and Kim.

"Ah..." Abbi started to speak and shut her mouth.

"Well, helloo Officer." Kim could clearly see how attractive the cop was. "You see, she's not in her right state of mind at the moment," Kim supplied, pointing to her head. She spun her finger in circles, silently conveying that Abbi was off her rocker. For good measure, she softly muttered "cuckoo", as she turned to look out her window.

The cop looked taken aback. "Is that so?" he asked searching Abbi's face.

Ava leaned across Abbi just then.

"What she means is, my mother... err... Abbi here," she jerked her head towards Abbi. "Has had quite a shock. You see, there was a plane crash..."

Frowning, he looked between Ava and Kim. The doubtful look on his face had Ava immediately clamping her mouth shut. She didn't want to say anything more in case the officer decided to haul them all off to jail.

"Then why is she driving, and not one of you?" he asked sourly.

"She didn't ask?" Kim supplied, thinking he was insane for even suggesting it. One didn't tell Abbi what to do when she was in this state of mind. She would bite their heads off if they did.

Abbi felt like a child at that moment. She had to say something, to fess up to her crime of speeding like a lunatic down the busiest highway in North America.

"Whoa, wait, hold up." Abbi held her hand up for some calm. She didn't feel very calm now, but she had to take control. "Officer. Wait, what is your name, again?" she asked scrunching her brow in thought. She was sure he'd mentioned it.

"I didn't say... Miss..." He pulled out a penlight, flashing the beam across her license.

Abbi was suddenly blinded by that same beam. She squinted from the onslaught of brightness.

"Abbi? Abbi Petersen, aka Abbi Stevens?"

She held up her hand, trying to shield her eyes. "Ahh... yes? Do I know you or something? Could you please get that light out of my face?" She blinked rapidly.

"Oh, shit... sorry. It's Noah. Noah Steel? We went to high school together." He grinned when the recognition hit Abbi's face.

With a squeal, Abbi grabbed the door handle, shoving it open, she unsuccessfully launched herself at Noah. Her seat belt halting her actions, momentarily slamming her back against the seat.

"Some things never change, do they Abbi?" Noah bellowed. "Here, let me give you a hand." He leaned in, reaching over he unsnapped her belt. Taking her hand, he guided her out of the vehicle and into his arms.

"*What?!*" Ava and Kim cried in unison, gaping at the couple as they embraced.

"Uh… Aunt Kim… are you seeing what I'm seeing?" Ava whispered in disbelief.

Kim just stared with her mouth agape.

Ava snapped her eyes to Kim. "Did you know about this and not tell me?" She hissed, before turning back to her mother embracing a stranger, well to her anyway.

"How the hell would I know? They… they seem to know each other. If you catch my drift," Kim stammered.

"Yeah. What do you think we should do?" Fearing she would miss something. Ava risked a glance at Kim again.

"I don't know…" Yanking on her door handle Kim said, "Let's go, we need to intervene."

"Wait for me!" Ava scrambled out her door, rounded the front of the SUV, and abruptly plowed into Kim's back.

"Jesus, Mary and Joseph," Kim muttered under her breath. There before them, stood Abbi and the officer… Noah, talking in hushed tones, soothing Abbi as she cried on his shoulder.

"No, no, no! This is not a good thing," Ava stated as she watched, shaking her head. She gave Kim a shove. "Stop them!"

"*Me*? Why me? She's *your* mother."

"You've known her longer. Besides, she's used to you butting in," Ava stated.

"Fine… but you're coming with me."

Together, they moved as one. Shifting from one foot to the other, Kim took a deep breath and said, "Ahem. Abbi, honey. We need to finish up here if you want to get to Ben. You do remember Ben... don't you?" Kim scooted closer, talking in a soothing tone.

Abbi swallowed, hard, her eyes red from crying. She backed away from Noah, wiping her tears off his jacket. She nodded, not trusting herself to speak just yet.

Kim had never seen Abbi so upset before in her life. She didn't know if Abbi was upset about Ben or from seeing Noah in her life again. Seeing how this was the first time Kim had the privilege of laying her eyes on the officer, she wasn't entirely sure what Noah meant to Abbi. One thing she was certain of was that it ended here and now.

Noah caught the emphasis on Ben's name. "Kim, is it?"

At her nod he continued. "Abbi was just telling me about Ben. I can understand why you guys are in a rush, that is why I offered to escort your vehicle to Windsor. I can only go as far as the Ambassador Bridge. But... on one condition." Noah looked at Ava and Kim.

Both had the 'caught in the headlights' look of a deer on the side of a darkened road.

"Noah doesn't want me driving." Abbi explained, finally breaking her silence.

"Of course not!" both women exclaimed, relief evident on their faces as they rushed over to hug Abbi.

"Then it's settled. I'll just radio into dispatch; explain the situation while you all go do your business in there." Noah pointed to the service station.

"I was afraid I'd have to get physical with you Noah... err... Officer... Noah. I'll just shut up now," Kim snickered. She really needed to learn to keep her mouth shut, she thought, as she felt the blush rise to her cheeks. "Well, you know... Abbi and Ben..." she tried to smooth her outburst over.

"I do, and Abbi and I have always been just friends. Right, Abbs?"

Abbi smiled and nodded. She still didn't trust herself to speak too much. And, felt like she was on the edge of a meltdown. That wouldn't do. She had to find Ben. Even if it meant... *NO! You are not going there, Abbi!! He is alive...*

"Come on, Mom, let's get something to eat." Ava put an arm around her, guiding her toward the building while Kim followed, staring at the police officer with a dreamy look in her eyes.

Abbi sat with her head in her hands at the table, waiting for Ava and Kim to return with their food. She laid her purse on the table and planted her face on it. She didn't care that people were shooting strange looks her way. She was so unbelievably spent. If she had the strength, she might have just shot them back a look or two... or given them the one-finger salute.

Abbi, that's not like you at all, she thought, as her purse vibrated against her face. *What the hell is that?* She sat up straight and rummaged through it to find the culprit. Her phone... She never had the sound on, let alone vibrate. Ava. She must have turned it on. Tapping the screen, she saw there were a couple of texts and 10 missed calls. She scrolled through the call log.

Thank you, God... It was Mark. With shaking hands, Abbi quickly stabbed his number. He picked up after the second ring.

"Mark, it's Abbi, is Ben with you?" She closed her eyes, waiting.

"Hey, Abbi. Uh, how's it going?" He sounded so... distraught. "Mark... where are you? Is Ben with you?"

"I guess you heard about the plane crash, huh?"

Why is he beating around the bush...? She took a calming breath. "Yes, I did. It's all over the news. But where are you now?"

"Me? I'm at the hospital. They are keeping me for observation... just for the night," he told her.

"Where is Ben? Is he with you?" She knew he wasn't, but she had to hear it before she would admit it to herself.

"Ben? Umm…"

"Spit it out for cripes sake or I'll rip you a new asshole when I see you next!" she shouted into the phone.

Her tirade caused everyone to look her way, including Ava, Kim, and Noah.

"Oh, oh…" Kim said with dread.

"I'm on it," Ava replied, as she spun on her heel, running towards her mom.

Abbi was apologizing to Mark for her outburst when Ava arrived at the table. She motioned for her to give her the phone.

"Mark, I'm so sorry. I need answers and no one seems to know them… Ava wants to talk to you." Abbi handed Ava the phone as she got up from the table. She headed to the washroom, the only place she could escape to. Pushing open the first stall door, she locked it and sat heavily on the toilet, bursting into tears.

Carrying a tray full of drinks, Kim scanned the eating area for Abbi as she made her way to the table where Ava sat, alone. "Where's your mom?" she asked, placing the tray on the table, as she looked around again.

"She went to the washroom. I just got off the phone with Mark." Ava said.

"And?" Kim hedged as she stuck straws in the drinks.

"He's in the hospital, just overnight… for observation. He should be released tomorrow if all goes well."

"Ok, so where did the plane go down?" Noah asked, dropping bags of food on the table.

"Mark was told about 60 miles south of Gatlinburg, Tennessee, near a little mountain town called Cooper's Hill."

"And... Ben?" Kim held her breath, waiting for the response. She didn't know what they would do with Abbi if it wasn't good.

Ava took a deep breath. "Ben is nowhere to be found." She said, looking at Kim and Noah.

"What do you *mean*, nowhere to be found?" Abbi cried in horrified disbelief. At the three shocked faces that peered at her, it was clear that no one had seen her return. Abbi thrust out a shaky hand "Give me my phone, Ava."

Concerned at her mother's current mental state, Ava passed her the phone. "Mom, Mark said he looked everywhere. And so, did the police. It's like he just vanished into thin air."

By that time, Abbi wasn't listening. She tapped her screen, going instantly to the text messages... *Ben.* He had sent her two. The first she read with tears swimming in her eyes...

'Abbi. Love. It's me. Things are not looking so good for Mark and me and I won't go into details. I know I have told you this before, but please, always remember that you captured my heart from the second we met. You are the best thing that has ever happened to me. I have no regrets with you, love. No matter what happens, know that I will always love you and I'll always be by your side. Forever yours, Ben.'

She had to sit down as a soft sob escaped past her lips. *There is another one Abbi, stay calm.* Taking a steadying breath, she continued to read the second one...

'Hello there, Abbi, I presume? I am not sure who this is. But from the last message I sent you, I am confident that we know each other... intimately. I seem to be in some need of assistance but have no idea where I am. Can you please advise? Thanks, Benjamin Quinn'.

Abbi started giggling. Softly at first, then full out laughing hysterically. It really wasn't funny, of course. Ben had no clue as to who she was, but she couldn't help herself. She knew it! He was alive!

"What's so funny?" Noah asked.

Between the tears slipping down her cheeks and her hysterical laughing, everyone at the table thought she had finally lost it.

"Ahh…" She wiped the tears away with her sleeve. "He's alive…" was all she managed to say.

"Mark is, yes… we know that mom."

Abbi shook her head; she shoved her phone to the center of the table. "Not Mark, Ava. Ben… he's alive," Abbi said as she broke down in sobs of relief.

༺༻

True to his word, Noah was in the lead, sirens blaring and lights flashing. They were en-route to Windsor, with Ava at the wheel, just passing through Chatham Kent.

Abbi texted Ben back, after multiple attempts to reach him by phone had failed. Twenty minutes later he had responded, telling her that he was injured. A broken leg, he was sure of, and he was slipping in and out of consciousness. Abbi had immediately called 911, telling them she was talking to Ben via text. They said they could contact his phone provider and narrow down the pings on the towers around the vicinity of the plane crash, but he had to make a call first. Her last text to him, she'd told him that it was imperative that he call her.

Abbi leaned her head back. She stared blankly at the night sky through the SUV's glass top roof, as it sped its way to their destination. Despite her protests, they'd decided to stay the night in Windsor; at least another forty-five-minute drive away. Luke and Lane were both out of town on business and so they had little choice but to stay in a hotel.

There was still 9 hours, possibly more of driving ahead of them in the States. She hated to waste time on sleeping. She would see. She may just leave in the middle of the night. She would sneak away like a thief in the night... without Ava and Kim.

Chapter 2

Ben woke with a start to find that a light dusting of snow covered him. *Where the hell am I? Now that's a question that may never get answered*, he thought wryly, as he laid a hand on his leg. He knew it was banged up bad, likely broken. He also knew that if he didn't get out of there and soon, he wouldn't make it. If only he could find something that resembled a crutch, maybe just may-be he could get the hell out of there. It would have to wait till day-light though. The moon barely gave off enough light to see through the leafless trees.

A twig snapping had him whipping his head around to the sound. Something was out there. He heard it, and he felt like he was being watched. Whatever it was, it didn't come close enough to get a good look at it. Likely a raccoon. He hoped. Then again, he could have just imagined it. His mind had been playing tricks on him, since the second he had woken up laying on the forest floor. The first time, he'd heard a woman's voice in his mind, made him think he was going crazy. Now, he looked forward to it.

He touched his fingers to the bump on his forehead, wincing from the pain. He tried to remember what had happened. He knew from the sickening screech of metal that played on repeat in his mind that he had been in a plane crash. From the looks of it, he had been the only occupant... or so he thought. It was the only thing he was certain of... that and his name.

Shivering against the cold, he closed his eyes, trying desperately to remember what his life was like. He had looked endlessly at the photos on his phone. There were pictures of a lake, a house in the middle of renovations, dogs. Pictures of him and a beautiful woman together, some of just her alone. He knew they were a couple; he could feel it in his gut, but he just couldn't remember her.

Abbi she was. The photo attached to her name and phone number told him so. He also knew deep down; she meant the world to him. Ben just wished he could remember her. The feel of her skin, her laugh, her voice, anything that would bring a hint of what he had meant to her. Did she love him? God, he hoped so. He could feel himself drifting off again. The image of Abbi burning into his mind was his last thought before sleep overtook him.

The buzzing of his phone had him jerking awake. It was Abbi. He squinted trying desperately to focus on the words in the text. *'Ben, please call me. I need you to call. The police can trace your cell off the towers. But you have to call.'*

He hit the phone icon as his teeth started to chatter. He waited shivering uncontrollably, praying the call would go through this time.

"Ben?"

He heard a soft voice in his ear. The same voice he had heard in his mind repeatedly.

Memories of her, of them, flashed through his mind "Abbi, is that you?" His voice broke on her name as it all came flooding back to him.

He could hear her crying softly. Like usual, her tears tore his heart out.

"Love, please don't cry. I'm fine. Just a bit banged up is all."

"You called me love, does that mean...?" she trailed off.

"Yeah, I remember. I could never forget you for long Abbi." He heard her let out a shaky breath, half laughing half crying.

Ben remembered how beautiful she was with tears streaming down her face. He wanted nothing more than to kiss them away.

"Mark is in the hospital in Gatlinburg. Ava and Kim have no idea, but I'm on my way to you. They'll know once they wake up. I'm headed to the Detroit airport right now. Hang on a second." He heard a sharp whistle, and her hailing for a taxi. A muffling sound came through the speaker as she told her destination to the driver. "I'm back. I should be there in an hour and a half. I don't know, maybe more," She panted, out of breath.

Ben had no idea who Mark was, and who was Ava and Kim? Hell, he didn't even know who his own family was, for that matter. Maybe they were his family? All he knew at this point was Abbi and she was coming for him.

"Wait, you're going to fly... alone?" he asked her.

Softly Abbi said, "Nothing is stopping me from getting to you."

The determination in her voice made his heart swell. Knowing what she was about to embark on, he loved her more in that moment than he had ever loved another.

Swallowing hard, he said, "Abbi, I'm about to pass out I think...." He lied, wanting to spare her from his emotions. He hated to end the call, but he had to.

"Ben... No!! Stay with me! Don't you dare fall asleep on me now!" she ordered.

He had to chuckle at the fire in her voice.

"Fine, Love, just keep talking to me. Tell me what you've been up to. I'll try to stay awake. It's just so bloody cold out here." He mumbled, just as he heard the crack of branches breaking. *Good god, I hope she didn't hear that...*

But apparently, she had because she screeched, "What the hell was that?!" into his ear. He could feel the panic in her voice rising with each word through the phone.

Lights blinded Ben. He had no idea what it was other than it was a vehicle with a loud muffler.

"Just one second love," he muttered, He quickly switched his phone to record, stuffing it and Abbi's muffled curses in his pocket.

"See Dean, I told you it was that Hollywood actor, sitting here in the middle of these here trees."

How the hell did they find me? All Ben could see in any direction was endless trees. Really at that point he didn't care, he would be back to civilization soon. He could make out two figures. The one talking, skinny as bean pole. The one called Dean, was tall as well but built like an athlete. Relief spread through Ben; he was saved. It came as a bit of a shock that they thought he was an actor though. The thought was absurd in his rattled mind.

"For once in your pathetic life Smitty, you're right. Come on. Let's get him loaded into the back of the truck." The one called Dean stalked over to Ben.

"Uh, how do you know me?" Ben asked the one named Smitty.

Smitty snorted. "Man, there isn't a person in the world who doesn't know who you are."

"I see." Ben said on a grimace as he was hoisted up by the armpits by both men.

"Can you walk?" Smitty asked, trying to steady Ben.

"How dumb can you be? The man has been sitting here for hours. If he could walk, he would have left by now." Dean spat out at his companion as he gathered debris from the plane wreckage.

Smitty shrugged his shoulders as he put an arm around Ben's waist. "Don't pay him no mind." he muttered under his breath. "He's just pissed you landed in the middle of our farm."

Ben glanced around as he hobbled to the pickup truck and frowned. *Farm? All I can see is barren trees for miles. What the hell kind of farm is Smitty referring to*, he wondered.

"Smitty, keep your trap shut." Dean growled as he brought up the rear. He walked to the bed of the truck and tossed his findings inside. Yanking open the driver's door, he grumbled, "We don't want Mr. Hollywood knowing anything... got it? Otherwise, he may just have to go missing again."

"I'm sorry," Smitty mumbled under his breath. He darted his eyes to Ben as he opened the door of the club cab for him. Both men knew what 'missing' meant.

Ben climbed into the backseat trying his damnedest to keep from bumping his leg. It was impossible for him not to grunt in pain when he settled on the seat.

"What's up with you?" Dean asked, turning to look at Ben.

With sweat beading on his brow, Ben pulled on his pant leg, tugging on it, he pulled his leg into the truck and said, "Busted my leg in the crash,"

Dean sent him a sour look. "Great, just what we needed."

"We can take you to the hospital," Smitty said to Ben. He looked to Dean for confirmation, "Right?"

"Nope. Too much of a risk, someone is bound to recognize him." Dean hissed.

"We can't leave him to suffer..." Smitty reasoned.

"We'll get Murdock to look at him." Dean said starting the truck. "If she can't set it, well that's just too bad, isn't it?" He put the truck in gear and backed up.

Ben looked around, as they sped through the forest. Trying to see anything he could to tell Abbi to use as a landmark. Trees and more trees met his eyes. Just his luck. His eyes grew large when he heard someone yelling from what sounded like far way.

What the hell? Shit, Abbi! He forgot she was still on the phone, no doubt hearing every word exchanged. Damn, she was going off on the other end. He quickly put his hand over his jeans pocket, fearing she would be heard. By feel, he disconnected the call, he hoped. He couldn't afford for the two in the front seat to know he had it. He needed his cell if he was ever going to be found.

The truck pulled up to what looked like an abandoned warehouse in the middle of the forest. *This does not look good.* There still wasn't a farm that Ben could see.

Dean killed the engine, looking over at Smitty, he jerked his head to the back seat where Ben sat.

"Get him inside, take him to Murdock. See if he can be fixed up."

"And if he can't? Then do we take him to the hospital?" Smitty asked.

"I don't know yet, I'll have to think about it. He should bring in a hefty price." Dean sneered.

Price? What the hell are they dealing here? Ben wondered.

"Right." Smitty nodded, as he opened his door and slammed it shut.

He came to Ben's door, opening it he said, "Come on, I'll get you looked at." Again, Ben couldn't help but groan in pain as Smitty helped him from the truck and to the building. The slightest movement of his leg made him want to vomit.

The smell caught Ben off guard. His first thought was that a family of skunks had taken up residence close by. As they drew closer to the building, the smell intensified.

Smitty guided Ben to a post. "Here, hang onto this while I open the door."

Ben gripped the post with one hand waiting for Smitty to open the door. He wished he could just take off running. But he had a feeling that if he attempted it, a bullet would find its way into the back of his head. Nope. Better to play it safe, he had Abbi coming for him.

Funny, how a few months ago he wouldn't have even cared. Holy shit! he remembered somewhat of his life before Abbi came into it. Merely existing. Amazing how she'd changed it, he thought, as Smitty shoved open the huge sliding door.

Ben's eyes grew large as light streamed from the open doorway. That wasn't a family of skunks he smelled a few minutes ago. That was the 'farm'. There stood before him, row after row, was the largest marijuana plants Ben had ever seen in his life. He let out a low whistle. He had no clue where he was but was fairly sure that what stood before his eyes was an illegal grow op.

"Bloody hell..." Ben said in shock. The seriousness of his current predicament hit him like a ton of bricks.

"Pretty impressive, huh?" Smitty asked smiling, as he closed the door with a loud bang.

"Indeed, it is." Ben returned as he watched a worker walking around with a gun. One that he was sure was loaded. *No. this wasn't good, not good at all.*

The stakes just got higher. He had to come up with a plan and damn quick if he was ever going to get out of this alive....

Chapter 3

"Ben! Please answer me! Damn it!!" Abbi screamed frantically into her phone. God, she felt so helpless. When she heard the crashing of trees and the sound of the vehicle, hope flared in her chest. She thought for sure the police had found him. That hope soon plummeted to her gut after hearing the voices. She held her breath as she heard them talk about Ben... not to him. Abbi instantly had a bad feeling about them. She had repeatedly called out to Ben, praying he would respond. The only one to hear her was the cab driver who was sending startled glances in the rear-view mirror at her.

"Can you step on it, please?" She pleaded with the cabbie as she listened to the muffled conversation on her cell.

"Sure thing, ma'am." The taxi shot forward as the driver stomped on the gas pedal.

"Sweet baby Jesus, not *that* fast. I need to get there in one piece." The driver mumbled an apology as he slowed down.

Abbi breathed a sigh of relief as the car reduced its speed to a more reasonable pace. She needed to call the police in Gatlinburg, but she dared not hang up on Ben.

"Ah, sir." Abbi tapped the driver on the shoulder. "Do you have a cell phone I can use?"

"Lady, you do realize you're talking on one, right?" He looked at her as if she had horns growing out of her head.

"Of course I do, but I can't just hang up on him!" She bit that out a little louder than she intended. *Calm your jets Abbi, he has no clue what's going on...*

She tried again, more calmly this time, "I'm sorry to ask but it's a matter of life and death!" She saw the doubt he cast her way in the rear-view mirror.

"Look, my boyfriend was in a plane crash in the middle of butt fu... um a forest. He's been missing since yesterday morning. And these..." she waved her hand about, as if she were at a loss for the correct term "... people showed up."

"Well, that's a good thing, right?"

"Yes, ... *No!*!" She denied vehemently. "They aren't there to help him! They're there to take him!!" She was close to snapping.

"How can you be so sure? I mean, if it were me, and people showed up I would be pretty damn happy to see them... Wouldn't you?" The cabbie reasoned.

Shaking her head, she all but yelled. "Yes! If they were the right people, *but these people aren't the right people!*" she ended with a hurried hiss.

He gave her a confused look; she had to explain.

"I know this because, I heard them. They are going to sell him or kill him... I'm not sure which. But whatever it is, it's not a good thing." She paused, listening into her phone to what sounded like Ben groaning in pain. *"Oh my God, what the hell are they doing to him?"*

"Lady, I think you're overreacting."

Me overreact?

Abbi wasn't that person to throw her name around to get what she wanted. In fact, she never did. But this was calling for drastic measures.

"Look..." She squinted in thought, "What was your name again?"

"It's Leo, but I never did tell you my name." He smiled.

Huh, he's a nice-looking man when he doesn't think I'm crazy, Abbi thought to herself.

"Leo, my name is Abbi Stevens." She used her pen name in hopes he would recognize it. She held her hand out by way of introduction.

Never taking his eyes off the road, he reached over and took her hand for a quick shake. "Nice to meet you, Abbi." He nodded; the smile was replaced with that 'this lady is crazy' look again.

Great, he has no clue who I am. She had no choice but to pull out the big guns.

"Ah, you see. My boyfriend… Ben Everett, you know, the actor?" She intentionally asked it as a question, waiting to see the dawning recognition his name would bring to Leo's face. It never happened. "The one that was in the plane crash, well… It's been all over the news I'm sure you heard by now."

"Nope, can't say I've heard of him and I don't listen to the news," he said, shaking his head.

Does this guy live under a rock on his off days?

"Ok." Abbi counted to ten. "How about movies, do you watch movies?"

"Sure do! I don't tell people this because they would think I'm crazy, a big bear of a guy like me. But seeing how you're crazy already, I'll tell ya. I do love a good chick flick." Leo grinned at her reflection in the mirror.

Rolling her eyes, she said, "Of course you do…" Abbi flung herself back against the seat, letting out an exasperated sigh of de-feat. Knowing the fact that Ben had never been in a movie made for women, Leo wouldn't know him even if he was standing in the same room.

She tuned him out, straining to hear any sign that Ben was still connected to her. A rumbling, squealing noise came over the airwaves. That didn't sound good...

She was trying to picture what could have made that noise when Leo's prattling broke her thoughts.

"Now, that Mark Donovan, he's quite the character." He laughed smacking his knee.

Yes! This was her chance to seize the moment. She leaned forward, all but hanging over the front seat. "Mark!!! I know him!! He rents out my house."

"Sure, he does lady." Leo replied cynically.

"He does!" Taking the phone from her ear, Abbi swiped through her photos, careful not to disconnect her call. Finally, she found one of Mark, with Ava and Kim.

Shoving it under his nose she said, "Here, look. That's him with my sister and daughter."

"Whoa, hang on a minute, let me pull over before I crash into something." Leo signaled, pulling off to the shoulder, safely pulling to a stop.

Putting the cell back to her ear, Abbi grabbed the door handle, and shoved it open. Kicking it shut, she yanked open the front door and planted her butt on the seat. She would get better results if she were eye to eye with the man.

Leo jumped back in his seat, surprise registering on his face. Abbi threw him a smile as she settled in and closed the door with a soft thud.

She could tell he wasn't too sure about her now.

Shooting her a wary look, Leo motioned with his hand, "Ok, let me see your phone."

She had heard nothing for a while, but just in case, she switched the speaker on so that she could listen for Ben while they scrolled through her photos.

"Huh... so you do." Leo shrugged, "So, what's he really like?" he asked.

"Wouldn't you like to know." Abbi said airily, folding her arms across her chest. She leaned back and looked out her window.

He nodded at her phone as he pulled away from the curb. "Look Abbi, you can't just show me these, and just leave me hanging," he said looking at her, he noted her defiant stance. "Fine! Okay!! I'll let you use my phone, but only if you tell me."

Abbi stuck her hand out. "Phone first, then I tell you everything you want to know."

"Deal." He said passing her the phone. She greedily took it, quickly calling the Gatlinburg Sheriff's office.

Abbi had just finished telling Leo about Mark when he pulled the cab to stop at the curb outside of the airport.

"Well, it was real nice chatting with you Abbi. You got my number, right?" Leo asked her for the tenth time.

I bet it was, Abbi thought, nodding in answer to his question. She had told him everything about Mark, right down to his favourite food. She would have to tell Mark that she was sorry... like, really sorry.

Somehow Leo had not only gleaned every detail out of her, but he swindled a promise of a trip to Pearl Lake to meet Mark when everything was sorted out.

"It was nice talking to you too Leo, thanks again for letting me use your phone," She tossed a couple of crisp one hundred-dollar bills at him before slamming her door shut.

"Hey Abbi, you gave me too much," Leo protested.

"I know I did, keep the change," she tossed over her shoulder, waving as she ran inside.

Moonlit Road

She quickly ran up to the attendant, paid for her ticket and ran to catch her flight. If all went well, she would be in Tennessee within an hour or so. She could only hope she didn't end up running down the aisle like the crazy woman Leo thought she was.

Abbi hoped she appeared calm and confidant to others. That was the furthest thing from the truth. Her feet felt like they wanted to take root, she felt the weight of anxiety with every step she took. Wanting nothing more than to turn around and head back to the safety of the terminal; she forged on; she had to… Ben needed her.

Taking a deep breath, she planted herself in her seat and buckled the belt as tight as she could. *As if this flimsy thing will save me,* she thought as her stomach churned.

She sent a silent prayer to the gods that be. Praying that the plane would stay in the air and that she wouldn't make a complete ass of herself. Leaning back, she closed her eyes. Memories of the last time she had flown came flooding back. It was to Madrid with Ben. He was needed back to film the last scenes for the Jasper Killings, and oh what a time she had on that flight…

She had been drunk, of course. He made sure she stayed in her seat the whole time. He even went as far as holding her when she started keening like a baby and held her hair as she threw up in the aisle. Tears fell silently down her cheeks. Missing him was one thing, but him being taken somewhere only God knew, was slowly tearing her apart, second by second.

"Just where the hell do you think you're going?"

Abbi cracked an eye open at the familiar voice. Only to discover Kim, Ava and an out of uniform Noah, all gaping at her from the aisle.

"Mom, are you crazy? You can't fly alone." Ava said taking the seat beside her.

"I can so." Abbi felt like a child being scolded. To be honest, she was relieved to see them. She hadn't really wanted to take to the skies alone. Or at all for the matter.

"How did you find me, anyway? And Noah? You can't just leave work," she said tiredly.

"Sure, can Abbi, I'm on vacation as we speak. What better way to spend it than looking for a missing person?" He smiled.

Kim jerked her thumb at Noah. "Mr. Cop here... followed us from the hotel," Kim said as she took her seat. "We flew past you on the way here. Surprised you didn't see Ava waving at you like a fool, hanging out the window like she was."

Abbi took Ava's hand, giving it a squeeze. "Well, thanks for coming. I didn't want to wake you two up, that's why I snuck out."

"Snuck out?" Kim snorted. "Is that what you call it? Cussing and muttering to yourself as you banged out the door, isn't exactly how one would sneak."

The pilot's voice came over the speaker announcing takeoff just then. Abbi gripped the arms on her seat, leaned back and bit her lip as sweat beaded on her brow. She squeezed her eyes tightly shut. *Okay, Abbi calm the hell down, it's only for a few minutes and then it'll even out.*

"Hang in there, mom, I'll get you a nice stiff drink in a minute," Ava told her in a soothing tone.

"You should have started drinking when you left the hotel," Kim cackled. For some reason, she always thought it was hilarious how Abbi reacted to flying.

Abbi clenched her jaw, muttering out the side of her mouth she said, "Will you just shut the hell up, Kim."

The plane finally evened out, allowing her to relax the grip she had on the seat. Thank God it was a short flight. When she got Ben back, they were driving home... alone.

Chapter 4

Smitty grabbed Ben by the arm and wrapped it around his shoulders. "Come on, I'll get you over to Murdock. See if she can help your leg." He guided Ben to a short hallway. Taking a left, they came to a doorway at the end of the hall.

"Hey Murdock," Smitty called out. "Got a minute? This guy needs looking at."

Ben saw a tiny woman who had to be at least eighty, hunched over a microscope. He doubted she could patch him up; she looked so weak and nothing like a doctor. She turned just then, scrutinizing him over her glasses. She motioned with a wave of her hand at the table sitting in the middle of the room.

"Help him up."

Ben swallowed hard. Bloody hell, her voice sounded as old as she looked. He wasn't entirely sure he trusted her but had little choice. The pain was blinding; every move had him fighting consciousness and the urge to vomit.

"What's your name boy?" she asked as she shuffled over to him.

"Ben," he answered, grimacing as he pulled his leg up and onto the table. He could feel the beads of sweat forming on his upper lip at the effort. Heaven help him he felt like sawing his own leg off.

"My name's Daisy, Daisy Murdock. Now let's have a look see," she said, turning towards him with a pair of scissors. She made fast work of cutting his pants at the ankle, clear up to his

Moonlit Road

hip. She let out a low whistle, nearly spitting out her dentures, in the process.

"Oh, hell, No!" Daisy said. "Smitty, go tell Dean there's no way I can fix that." She backed away, shaking her head. Quickly she ran behind Ben, hurling into the nearby sink as Smitty took off out the door gagging.

What the hell kind of doctor can't set a leg? Ben wondered. He looked down at it. Aside from it being bloody from a scrape and bruised, it wasn't that bad. Sure, the bone bulged against his skin, but at least it hadn't poked through... yet. Yeah it was gross, but Ben had seen worse. Something was off with this doctor.

"Um, Daisy? You okay?" Ben twisted around to get a look at her face.

She cleared her throat. "Yeah, what makes you think I'm not?" She snapped.

Ben pursed his lips. "Oh, I don't know... Maybe tossing your cookies at the sight of my leg has me wondering."

Daisy wiped her mouth with the back of her hand.

Ben noticed something very odd about her. "Huh..." he said, squinting in thought.

"What?!" She squeaked. "Why are you looking at me like that?"

"Your hands." He nodded towards them. "They don't match your face."

Ben was certain that Daisy Murdock was not who she claimed to be. In fact, he would bet on it. For one, her voice suddenly changed from the soft whispers of an old lady to a young, scared woman. He had to admit, her appearance was very convincing though. To the untrained eye, one would never be able to tell. Too bad for her that he'd seen right through it. *Wait a second, how the hell do I know that?* He frowned, searching what little memory he had. Nothing.

Daisy interrupted his thoughts. "Look, I know who you are," she said quietly.

Ben shot her a brooding glance. "You do?"

"Yeah, who doesn't?" Daisy silently moved to the door, closing it softly. Turning to look at him she said, "You're Ben Quinn. Everyone, at some point in their life, has seen a movie you're in."

Ben just sat there nodding, he had no clue if she were right, his memory just wouldn't reach back that far.

"You have no clue, do you?" Daisy asked. Reaching up, she grabbed his chin, turning his head to look at the bump on his forehead.

"Is it that obvious?" He'd need to work on that. If she could tell, then so could the others. He couldn't risk them finding out. Doing so, would put him in more of a perilous situation than he already was.

"Mhm" she said, walking over to a cupboard, she took the first aid kit and returned to his side.

Soaking a cotton ball in peroxide, she said "This will sting."

"Go ahead, it can't hurt any worse than my leg."

She wiped the bump so hard, it felt like she was trying to flatten it with the cotton.

He winced. "Bloody hell woman! Can you not do that? Give it to me. I'll do it myself." Ben said taking the cotton ball from her. Baiting her, he said. "You know, for someone so old, you have a heavy hand."

Daisy gave a tight smile. "Ah about that…"

Ben held up his hand. "No need to say a word. The less I know the better."

The door opened and in stepped Smitty with Dean close on his heels. The old woman in Daisy suddenly returned.

"Murdock, Smitty says you can't set his leg?" Dean barked.

"Take a look at it and ask me that question again," she retorted.

Dean moved over to where Ben was on the table, all color drained from his face.

"Well, shit!!"

"I told you it was bad," Smitty said to Dean, his eyes never wavering from the sight of Ben's leg. "He needs a hospital and fast," he stated the obvious.

"Well, he's not going anywhere tonight." Dean looked Ben in the eyes. "You're damn lucky Smitty and Daisy found you out there earlier. There's a freak snowstorm happening out there right now. No one would have found you in time."

Found me earlier? Ben wanted to question that but kept his mouth shut.

"I can wrap it but that's about it. He's likely going to need surgery for that bone." Daisy nodded, her eyes growing large as she took in the bruising on Ben's skin. She tore her eyes away to get a tensor bandage. Turning to Ben, she said, "I should probably take your boot off, do you think you can handle the pain?"

Ben nodded.

"Lay back, in case you pass out," she told him. She barked out orders. "Smitty, hold his thigh down, Dean hold his shoulders."

Daisy quickly undid his boot, slowly she slipped it off his foot. It felt like ice. She grabbed a pen and ran it along the underside of Ben's foot. "Can you feel that?" she questioned him.

"I feel a slight tingling sensation. Why?"

Daisy looked at Dean and shook her head. Smitty caught the exchange between the two. He could see the panic in Ben's face. "Uh, nothing, buddy, you're gonna be fine, isn't he Murdock?"

She shook her head no but said "Yeah, just fine." She quickly wrapped his leg from foot to thigh. He hardly had any feeling in his foot. She was no doctor, but she knew enough to know that Ben was possibly in serious trouble.

"So now what?" Smitty asked. "Where is he gonna bunk tonight?" He looked at Dean for an answer.

Daisy spoke up. "He's staying with me for the night in my cabin. I... Uh... I need to monitor him."

None of the men made a noise about that. Ben knew there was something wrong with his leg, but serious enough to need surgery... he highly doubted that.

To have no feeling, just a slight tingle in his foot was not right, especially when Daisy had a heavy hand. But he could feel his pulse and it just did happen. Of course, it would be numb for a few days at least.

"Help Ben sit up" Daisy said to the two men. "I've got some crutches in the supply room. Go get them, will you Dean."

That wasn't a request but an order, Ben noticed. *What is she? The boss of this operation?*

"Smitty, I'll need your help getting him to my cabin. He can use the crutches, that is, if he has the strength."

She looked to Ben. "You do have the strength, don't you?"

"Yeah, I'll be fine," he said, nodding. He wanted nothing more than to get the hell out of here to the cabin. He was in dire need of food and a decent sleep.

"Good. But just in case, Smitty you can be there to pick him up if he falls."

Helping Ben off the table, Smitty said, "Sure thing Murdock. I'll be right by his side."

Moonlit Road

"Come on then, let's get out of here." Daisy grabbed a jacket and gently pulled it on as if she were in a great deal of pain. She led the way, down the hall and to the left. Pushing the door open, she was almost thrown back from the force of the wind. Blowing snow blinded them momentarily as they all filed outside.

"Follow me!" Daisy shouted over the howling wind. Ben hobbled after her with Smitty bringing up the rear.

One step at a time, Ben repeated like a mantra in his mind. His arms felt like they would give out any second. The crutches slipped a few times but was able to catch himself before falling face first into the snowdrifts. Daisy finally reached the small cabin, she flung the door open, holding it for the two men to enter.

"Damnation! This weather is nuts." she said slamming the door closed behind them.

Ben chanced a look around. The room was rustic and simple. A small fireplace sat squarely against one wall with a sofa opposite. A small kitchen area with a table and two chairs sat off to one side. Ben could see two doors, leading to what he presumed was a bedroom and bathroom.

"Calvin, can you help Ben over to the table there?" Daisy said as she threw a newspaper-wrapped log into the fireplace and lit a match to it.

Ben gawked at her then at Smitty. *Wait... did I just hear her right? Who the hell is Calvin?*

"Sure thing, Sam. Here Ben, take a seat." Smitty pulled out a chair, as Ben sat down with a heavy sigh.

"Want a coffee?" Smitty asked as he filled the kettle. "I'll make you something to eat too. You must be starved."

Daisy sat down opposite Ben. She looked to Smitty. "I'll take a coffee too please," she murmured as she picked at her jawline.

For a minute, Ben thought he was hallucinating. First, the two were calling each other by different names and now it looked like Daisy was pulling her face off.

Ben rubbed his eyes; he knew he was extremely tired, or maybe he was asleep, and this was all just a nightmare?

Nope, he wasn't sleeping. Her face was now bare. And what it revealed was a pretty girl with a sprinkling of freckles across her cheeks.

He watched in disbelief as she pulled out a set of fake teeth, tossing them in a water filled bowl that sat in the middle of the table. With revulsion, Ben gawked as water splattered on its surface.

Daisy glanced at him. The look on his face must have been priceless because she burst out laughing, "Sorry about this, but we need to have a chat."

Ben nodded in agreement. This was getting more bizarre by the second….

Chapter 5

A short hour later their, flight was taxiing down the runway at the Gatlinburg airport. Abbi surprisingly wasn't drunk. Perhaps a little tipsy, but not drunk. After knocking back a shot of gin and a glass of wine, she felt somewhat capable of handling the flight. That was until they were met with a little turbulence half-way through. For the rest of it, she sat there with her head between her knees, ready for impact at any second. Impact from what, she wasn't entirely sure, but at least she was ready.

"Mom? Are you okay?" Ava asked, rubbing her back soothingly. "You can sit up now. We are almost at the terminal."

Abbi sat up and leaned back in her seat.

"Abbi what the hell happened to you?" Kim chuckled.

"What?!" She said a bit too loudly.

"Here, look." Kim laughed as she passed her phone to her.

Abbi saw in the mirrored back of the cell, her reflection. Her hair looked like she had been sitting on the wing of the plane the entire flight. The little makeup she had on was now smudged. She looked like a windswept clown and she didn't care.

"Meh, I really don't care at this point," she said passing Kim her phone back as she gathered her purse and carry on. All she cared about was finding Ben.

"Let's go." She said with determination, oblivious to the snickers and giggles from fellow passengers as she passed by.

She was on a mission, ready to go trek in the forest the second they were off the plane.

☼

They had checked into a hotel close to the hospital and were now walking to the nurses' station on the floor Mark's room was on. They had no idea if they were even allowed to come at such a late hour, but they had to try. Noah had gone to the local sheriffs to find out as much information he could on where the plane had crashed.

His plan was to make a map of the area and backtrack from the crash site.

"Excuse me, could you tell me which room Mark Donovan is in?" Ava asked.

Abbi glanced over to see a woman sitting at a low desk; clearly ignoring Ava.

"Move over Ava," Kim bristled. "Hi there!" she said. "We're here to see Mark Donovan. What room is he in?" Kim tapped the counter impatiently, trying to get her point across.

The nurse glanced up. "He's in a private room and is not having any visitors. Especially at midnight," the nurse answered, tiredly she pointed to the clock on the wall.

The nurse went back to her computer screen, making Abbi fuming mad. At this point, she had had enough. Nudging Kim aside, she stepped forward. "Look lady, we have travelled all the way from northern Ontario and Mark is expecting us. So, if you don't want us to go into each room looking for him, waking people up, you better tell us what room he's in."

The nurse, clearly annoyed, looked up at Abbi…and let out a small gasp.

Moonlit Road

"Abbi Stevens?" suddenly, the nurse looked at her in awe as she came to a half stand.

Abbi blinked a few times before she sharply asked, "What?"

Kim elbowed her in the ribs, while she jerked her head towards the nurse. "Ah... Why yes, I'm Abbi Stevens." She pasted a charming smile on her lips, "And you are?"

"My name's Cindy. I'm a huge fan of the Jasper Killings. Can you sign my book? I have it right here." Cindy quickly rummaged in her bag, producing the book along with a pen.

Surprised at how fast Cindy could move when she wanted something, Abbi said, "Ah, sure," as she took both and scribbled her name. "Look, I'm sorry for my outburst a minute ago, it's just been a really long day."

"Of course! I understand completely," Cindy said, bobbing her head, a huge grin plastered on her face as she glanced at Abbi's signature.

"What room did you say Mark was in again?" Abbi asked sweetly, knowing full well she didn't say.

Cindy hurriedly came around the counter. "He's in room 304. Here let me take you ladies right to him. I'm sure he will be happy to see you."

"How kind of you," Kim sneered.

Abbi shot her a look, silently conveying to Kim to shut the hell up.

Following Cindy down the hall, they made their way to a set of double doors marked 'Private'. She scanned her key card and pushed a door open, holding it for them to join her. As they continued down the hall, Abbi glanced at each open doorway, half expecting to see Mark there lying in a bed. Finally, they came to a stop; room 304. The nurse gave a quick rap with her knuckles on the gleaming wood. "Mr. Donovan, are you decent? You have some visitors." Cindy smiled opening it wide for them to enter.

"Thank you, Cindy for being so helpful." Abbi smiled.

"Yes! Thank you *so* much!" Kim couldn't help but add sarcastically.

Cindy nodded and quietly closed the door behind her.

"Did you really have to be such a bitch to her?" Abbi bit out.

"Look who's talking Miss *'Look lady, we've travelled blah blah blah'*." Kim laughed.

"Enough!!" Ava said, cutting in between the two of them, her eyes flashing daggers.

"Ladies."

All eyes turned to the man in the bed.

"Oh my God, Mark! We're sorry, it's been an awfully long trip." Ava said, rushing over to give him a hug.

For once, Kim had the decency to look ashamed. "Hey Mark," she gave him a small wave. "How you are doing?"

"Good, good." He nodded, the smile not quite reaching his eyes.

Abbi at that moment had never felt so empty. Yes, she was happy to see Mark, to see him alive and well. But heaven help her, it hurt so damn much knowing that Ben wasn't there with him. Tears started to well in her eyes.

Mark held his arms wide. "Come here, sweets."

She walked to his bed in a daze, collapsing in his arms as her body wracked with sobs.

"I'm so sorry Abbi. I searched for him everywhere. I couldn't find him. It's like he just disappeared." Mark's voice broke. "One way or another, come tomorrow we are going to go look for him. I promise," he said.

Abbi nodded. Pulling away, she sniffled. "It's okay. I know you looked for him." She wiped her tears away with her sleeve. It just occurred to her Mark didn't know she had talked to Ben.

She gave him a watery smile. "He's alive Mark."

A pained look crossed over Mark's face. "Abbi. You know that may not be the case, right?" he asked gently.

"No. He really is. Ben sent me a text. He didn't know who I was but knew from our conversations that I meant something to him. He called me, too." She began to pace. The relief she felt when he called her 'Love'. He remembered... how... she had no idea; but the feeling of hearing him say it, was one she couldn't put into words. It moved her so much.

"That's fantastic news!" Mark was ecstatic. "What did he say? Did he say where he was?"

She stopped to look at him. "No, he didn't say where he was. I think in the middle of a forest." She began to pace again. "Someone has him. I heard them come through. It sounded like a big truck plowing down branches trees." She heaved a sigh and looked at Ava and Kim, "I didn't tell any of you this. But whoever took Ben... it didn't sound good. He can't walk."

"What do you mean he can't walk?" Kim asked, frowning as she sat down in a chair.

"He said his leg is broken. And I assumed he must have hit his head because he didn't remember me at first." She said rubbing her own forehead as she paced the floor.

"Anyway, there were two guys talking... Smitty and Dean. They didn't talk to him, but about him. The one seemed like he wanted to help... Smitty I think it was, wanted to take him to a hospital. Dean said that Murdock could look at him..." She trailed off. Not wanting to repeat what she'd heard for fear of it coming true.

"And???" They all said in unison.

Abbi turned to look at them. All raised expectant eyes at her. "And..." She swallowed hard, trying so desperately to push the swell of tears down her throat. "There was mention of a farm. I'm not sure what kind of farm would be in a forest?" She was stalling; she knew it. Deciding that there was no reason to not tell

Moonlit Road

them, she simply said, "And Dean said, 'We don't want Mr. Hollywood knowing anything, or he may just go missing again'. The way he said missing, he didn't mean missing..." Suddenly, she felt sick.

Abbi ran to the door tucked into the wall, shoving it open, she prayed it was a washroom. She sent a silent thank you as she fell to her knees. Clinging to the toilet as she retched her guts out. Shakily, she sat on the floor, hugging her knees to her chest. God, she hated throwing up in a toilet, especially a strange one.

She pulled her cell phone from her pocket and opened her texts to Ben. She so wanted to call him but didn't dare. If someone heard his phone ring, or heard him talking, she was sure they would take it from him. It was 2 am and she needed to sleep; otherwise she would be of no use to anyone. She decided to send him a quick text; he always left his cell on vibrate; it would be safe.

'Ben, It's Abbi. We are here in Tennessee. Just leaving Mark's hospital room, will text you once we get to the hotel. Please be safe. I miss you dreadfully. Love Abbi'

She hit the send button and she stood up, opening the door she said, "Guys I need some sleep and I'm sure Mark does, too."

"Yeah, sure thing Abbi," Kim said. "Mark, we will come by in the morning to get you, okay?"

"I'll be here." He nodded as her and Ava went out into the hall. "Abbi. Can you look in my jacket pocket it's hanging in the closet." He motioned with his hand at the door to the right of his bed.

"Um... sure. What am I looking for?" she asked, looking at him as she pulled the door open.

"A box, a small one... But don't look in it." He rushed to say.

Abbi looked at him, confusion etched on her face.

"Promise me you won't open it," Mark said.

Her hand closed around the box and froze. She gave a quick nod. "I promise, Mark." She pulled her hand from his jacket and looked down at what it held. There in the palm of her hand was a small black box. One that would hold a ring…

"Mark. I can't…" she trailed off, shaking her head, tears springing to her eyes.

"Abbi… yes you can," he softly said. "I made a promise to Ben. That no matter what…" He stopped, swallowing back the tears. "You just hold on to that until you see him again, and I know you will. Then, you give it to him."

Abbi nodded. It's what Ben wanted. Otherwise, he would never have given it to Mark. "Okay. I can do this." her voice betrayed her, breaking on the last word. She made her way to the door, then stopped looking back towards the bed.

"Mark? It's not your fault, you know that, right?" She knew he was feeling guilty.

"Yeah I know. I'll see you in the morning, Abbi." He turned away to look out the window at the night sky.

"Right, I'll see you in the morning." She walked out the door to join the others waiting in the hall.

Mark couldn't help but feel guilty. The memory of his last moments with Ben, his words, echoing in his mind.

"I had to send Abbi a text. To tell her one last time that I love her."

He had scoffed at Ben. He had been having his own doubts, but to hear Ben voice them…

"Man, everything will be fine. We will be back home in no time. And you can ask her to marry you, just as you planned."

They had hugged then. He had felt Ben put something in his pocket, he had known what it was. His eyes flashed to Ben's with a questioning look.

"Promise me you'll give that to Abbi… if I don't make it."

"Come on Ben don't talk like that. You keep it..."

"Promise me Mark."

Had Ben had a premonition?

"Sure buddy, I promise..."

After what Abbi had said she'd heard, he wasn't sure they would find Ben. If he were found, would he be alive?

Chapter 6

"Here, Ben." Smitty passed him a steaming mug, as he set a plate of sandwiches on the table.

"Thanks man. So, uh... do one of you mind telling me what's going on?" Ben asked, reaching for a sandwich.

"Well, as you can see, we are sitting smack dab in the middle of a grow op... an illegal one, I might add." Daisy sighed, looking to Smitty. At his nod, she continued. "And we aren't who we appear to be."

Ben squinted, chewing thoughtfully. *Who the hell are these people?*

Smitty cleared his throat. "If we tell you who we are... you have to play along."

Ben pursed his lips. "Sure. Why not? It can't get any worse." He noticed the dark look pass across Smitty's face.

Great, just, great. "Okay... It can, can't it?" Ben looked between Smitty and Daisy for confirmation.

Both nodded slowly. Daisy got up and went to check the windows and doors. Making sure all was locked tight, she turned to Ben.

"I'm Special Agent Sam Perkins with the FBI." She inclined her head towards Smitty. "And that is Special Agent Calvin Falls with the US Marshalls. As you've probably guessed, we are working undercover. Have been for roughly four months."

Calvin spoke up. "It's vital that you remember to use our fictitious names."

"Then why the hell did you tell me!" Ben exclaimed.

"When your plane went down. Our agencies put the call out for us to be on the lookout for any missing passengers. All have been accounted for but you Ben. And given your celebrity status, we decided it was in your best interest…" Sam paused, taking a deep breath, she continued. "We believe your plane was targeted". She held up a hand when Ben was about to speak.

"Why? … At this moment we have no idea." She sighed. "It just so happened that it went down close to the farm. In a way, you're lucky we are here. Otherwise, God knows what would have happened had Calvin not found you."

Ben was getting a headache, he tried rubbing the tension from his neck and stopped. Looking up he said, "Wait… this makes no sense at all. Why would someone target a plane; the plane that I was on?"

He watched them exchange a look. They were holding something back; he had to find out.

"Look, I know there is more than you're telling me. If it's something to do with me I think I have a right to know," he stated.

Calvin raised his hands and backed away. "This is your department," he said to Sam.

"Don't remind me," she sighed, looking at Ben. "The FBI was informed two months ago, that there was a possible hit put on you."

Ben let out a bark of laughter. "Yeah, okay," he said. When he saw the serious look on her face, the laughter turned to shock, then rage. "And I'm just finding this out now?"

Sam winced. "Well, yeah." She nodded. "We investigated it of course, but it was unfounded. Look, this may all just be a coincidence. But the investigation needs to be opened again. For now, your safe here with us. And as soon as we can get you out of here safely, we will. Now, do you know of any reason someone would want you dead?"

Ben scratched his head. He was at a loss for words and so exhausted. "I have no idea," he said stifling a yawn. He cleared his throat, not wanting to admit he had no real recollection of his life other than Abbi. "What I do know is that I need sleep, and now."

"Here, I'll give you a hand," Calvin said coming to Ben's aide. Holding his chair for him to stand up, Calvin jerked his head to the wall with the two doors. "The one on the right is the bathroom." Hurrying over to the other door, he shoved it wide, "And this one is the bedroom."

"Guide me to the bathroom, would you mate?" Ben puffed. He hated to admit it but he felt like a newborn; he was so weak.

Calvin mumbled an apology. "Hang on, let me grab your crutches."

Ben waited and thought, *I need a plan. But first I need to take a piss then face plant on the bed and sleep for 12 hours.* Calvin came to him with the crutches in hand. Just as Ben went to take them, he felt his phone vibrate in his pocket. He paused. *Should I check it now?* Something just didn't seem right about any of this. He couldn't pinpoint it, but something was off.

Ben ignored his phone and hobbled his way to bathroom. Closing the door, he decided he'd wait until he was safely in the bedroom before checking it. He imagined that it was Abbi... Man how he missed her. He needed to get out of this place and back to her, but knew it was best to wait for an ally. There was no way he could get far on his own.

Banging his way out of the bathroom, Ben looked to both agents. "Uh... I'm gonna head to bed," he said, jerking a thumb towards the closed door. "That is, if we're through here?"

Sam nodded. "Yeah, go ahead. We'll talk more in the morning. Have a goodnight."

Moonlit Road

"Thanks, you too." Ben nodded as he headed into the bedroom.

He closed the door behind him. By the light of the moon, he felt for a lock on the doorknob. *Damn there isn't one.* He glanced around the sparse room, looking for something, anything, he could push against the door. His glance fell to the spot beside him and saw a chair. Leaning one crutch against the wall, he took the chair and wedged it under the doorknob. He didn't trust either of them to not come in during the night. Hobbling over to the bed he dropped the other crutch with a bang. Flopping onto it, he pulled his cell out of his pocket before he passed out.

There was a text from Abbi. Tears sprang to his eyes as he read it. She was close. God, he needed to hear her voice. Dialing her number, he waited for the call to connect.

"Ben?" He heard her say his name hesitantly, as if she wasn't sure it was him.

"Hello, Love," he whispered. "I'm alone in a bedroom," he said, glancing around the moonlit room. "I can't say too much… just in case they are listening."

"Oh Ben, I was so worried," she sobbed. "I heard them take you, and you groaning in pain. What did they do to you? Where did they take you, do you know?" Her words tumbled out faster than he could respond.

"Abbi, hold up," he said gently. "I just wanted to tell you how much I miss you… how much I love you…" he trailed off. He could hear her crying. "Aww love, please don't. I didn't mean to make you cry." He felt horrible now, knowing he wasn't there to kiss her tears away.

"I love you, too," she said softly, weeping.

"There's something I need to tell you. I remember nothing, except you Abbi. As far as I know, I remember everything about us, about what we shared… but no one else." He sighed. "Not even my parents, how crazy is that?" he asked, not expecting an answer. "From what they told me, I'm an actor. A popular one apparently... Whatever happens, know that you are the best thing that has ever happened to me. That, I'm certain of..."

"I'm coming for you, Ben, so please don't think like that. You're coming home with me and we will be home before Christmas. I don't care if I have to search every square inch. God help the person who gets in my way," she said with fiery determination.

Despite her crying, he had to smile at the passion in her voice. When she set her mind to something, come hell or high water, nothing stopped her.

"Now, tell me all you can about where they took you," she urged.

"It's a short distance from where I was... no more than a kilometre. It seems to be a compound of sorts." He paused, trying to think of anything he could that would help her. "There's a dirt road that leads to the main building, it's white... pretty close to the road, actually. And it smells like skunks."

"Skunks? That's a bit strange, don't you think?"

"Well, that's because it's pot plants, Abbi..." he responded.

"Pot plants?" he could hear the growing confusion in her voice.

"Yes. It's an illegal grow op, in the middle of nowhere." He sighed. "And Abbi... they have guns."

"Guns?" She yelled it so loud he worried they heard her in the other room.

"Hush, love! Yes, guns," he whispered.

"Oh God, Ben." He could hear the panic rise in her voice. He hated to mention the guns, but he knew Abbi, if she could, she would find a way to him. She needed to be warned.

"Listen, Abbi. I can't leave here on my own, at least not in this weather. There are two agents in the other room, one with the FBI and the other with the DEA. Now, this is important love.

Take these names down and find out if they are who they claim to be."

"Claim to be?" she squawked.

She's really getting worked up, he thought.

"Yes, something just doesn't sit well with me," Ben answered.

"Okay, I have a pen. What are their names?"

"Samantha Perkins, FBI and Calvin Falls, DEA. Do you think you can find out?" he asked.

"Yes, I'll get Noah to check them out for me. If they are who they say, then it shouldn't be a problem finding out."

That was a new name that came off her lips. "Noah? Uh... Who is Noah?"

"He's a cop, an old friend of mine. He pulled us over when I was speeding on the way down. He had some time off and is giving us a hand looking for you."

"You don't say..." Ben trailed off. Wondering just how close of a friend he was, to come all this way.

Abbi must have caught the tone of his voice for she said, "Don't worry, Ben. He's just a friend. Wild horses couldn't drag me away from you..."

"I miss you woman..." he murmured, tiredly.

"I miss you. More than you'll ever know," she whispered, her voice catching on the last word.

They both heard the tell-tale beeping of a cellphone that was on its last charge. Ben knew it was his. He likely shouldn't have called her, but he needed to hear her voice.

"Abbi, love, I need to go now," he told her.

"I know..." her voice broke, "I'm so sorry I didn't go with you when you wanted me to Ben. I should have gone."

Moonlit Road

"It's okay. I'm just happy it's me and not you. I wouldn't be able to cope as well as you, I'm afraid." he smiled. "I promise you, when this is all over and we are back home, I'm retiring." He could tell she was about to interrupt. "No, I'm serious Abbi, I'm done acting, clearly it's what got me into this predicament in the first place. And I don't ever want to leave you like this again."

"I can't argue with you on that," she gave a tired chuckle.

"Good," he murmured. He knew he should end the call, but he couldn't bring himself to do so. He wanted to hear her voice as he drifted off to sleep, to feel her satiny skin against his lips. He was torturing himself thinking of her like that. Needing to, he changed the subject.

"So, love, tell me. What do you want for Christmas?"

She laughed at that; it was so off the wall, he had to admit.

"You, Ben. Only you…" she said quietly.

Fighting to keep his eyes open, he said, "Abbi. I have no way to charge my phone, and I can't keep my eyes open. I have to go… goodnight my sweet one…" he murmured.

"Goodnight babe, I love you…" her voice echoed through his mind as sleep overtook him.

Chapter 7

They were all sitting in the hotel cafe eating breakfast. Abbi was on her fourth cup of coffee; she had decided to pass on the food. There was no way that she could stomach anything solid at that moment. She pulled a piece of paper from her pocket. Placing it on the table, she slid it across from her. "Noah, can you find out if these people are agents?"

"Sure thing," he nodded, stuffing a piece of toast in his mouth. Glancing down at the paper, he quickly looked up at her, a curious look in his eyes.

Abbi shivered, rubbing her hands up and down her arms, she looked around for the source of a sudden draft. There wasn't one. *Why am I so cold?*

She wrapped her hands around her mug, hoping its warmth would seep into her bones. "Ben has a bad feeling about them," she said, taking a sip of her coffee.

"No problem, I'll get right on it." He pushed away from the table. Taking out his cell, he walked a short distance away.

"Mark is expecting us to pick him up shortly. The doctor just discharged him." Ava leaned forward to look around Kim. "Um... mom, do you want to come with us or stay here and get some rest?" she asked, concern in her voice. Anyone in the room could see the toll this was taking on her mother.

Abbi glanced at her. Seeing Kim was about to put her two cents into the conversation, Abbi held up her hand as she stifled a yawn. She hurriedly said, "I'm coming." At their looks of worry, she added, "It's fine. Really, I'm fine. I got a few hours of sleep after I talked to Ben last night. Besides, Mark wants to get out to the site today and so do I." She wasn't fine, she was so utterly tired, but damned if she would admit it to them.

"Okay then. Let's go bust Mark out." Kim said, rising from the table.

As they gathered their belongings, Noah returned to the table.

"Abbi, I made a call to a friend of mine. He's going to check those names out and get back asap." He grabbed a muffin, peeling the paper off, he took a generous bite. "We ready to go, are we?" he asked, chewing around his words.

"Yes, first stop is getting Mark. Then we gas up and head out to the crash site," Kim said, heading towards the exit.

They were silent as they walked to the rental. Abbi scowled at the sky. The sun was trying desperately to break through the heavy snow clouds. It was going to be hard enough to find where Ben had crashed. More snow would make it a hundred times worse.

"I'll drive. Who has the keys?" Noah asked.

Without a word, Abbi tossed him the fob and climbed into the back seat with Ava. She needed to close her eyes for ten minutes. A cat nap was all she needed.

ಙಗ

Abbi jerked with a start. Glancing around, she saw trees in every direction. *Where the hell am I? Good Lord I've slept through.* She pulled her cell from her purse. Three hours had passed since leaving the hotel, and not a word from Ben. Yanking on the door handle, she shoved it open, and tumbled to the ground.

"Abbi, sweets! You're awake!" Mark came to her, helping her to stand. She closed the door leaning against the vehicle to get her bearings.

Moonlit Road

"Mark, I'm so sorry. I fell asleep." She stated the obvious.

Mark noticed the dark circles under her once bright eyes "Pfft... no worries. You needed the rest." He said softly.

Nodding, she silently agreed as her eyes took in the sight before her. Trees that had been scorched by flames that had long died out, now stood broken and battered. Plane wreckage was all around them. The realization hit her like a ton of bricks. It was unbelievable that anyone walked away from that. *More than one person didn't walk away, Abbi...* She shook her head to clear her thoughts. She couldn't think of that right now. She had to focus what energy she had on finding Ben.

"Mark... where did you stop looking for Ben at?" She asked unable to look away from the disaster before her.

"About a thousand feet in every direction." He sighed.

She headed towards the driver's side. "Okay. Noah?" she yelled. "Where are the keys?"

"In the ignition."

"Thanks." Pulling the door open Abbi said, "Mark, get in."

She jumped behind the wheel. Buckling her seat belt, she glanced at him. 'Which way was the plane coming from? And where was Ben sitting?" She raised her brows, waiting for him to answer.

"That way," Mark pointed as he pulled his seat belt around him. "And Ben had the window seat, towards the back of the plane. The one man that had passed away... uh... was sitting behind Ben. He was the last one I could find," he teared up at the memory. Abbi reached over and gave his hand a squeeze.

"Okay. Hang on. It looks like it might get a bit bumpy," she said, resetting the odometer. She wanted to keep track of how far they traveled.

Mark braced one hand on the dashboard and gripped the 'oh shit' bar with the other. He fought the panic that was gathering in his chest. She was right; it was damn bumpy. What made it worse was the fact that she was speeding down the middle of a forest. He refused to scream like a little girl going on her first roller coaster ride; despite wanting to. He chanced a glance at Abbi, she looked like she'd gone mad with her windswept hair and a crazed look in her eyes. *God, I hope she finds what she is looking for.*

Judging it to be a thousand feet, Abbi slowed down. Scanning every inch as they passed by, she looked for anything that might hold a clue. A piece of paper, wreckage from the plane... anything that would point to Ben being there.

"Does any of this look familiar?"

Mark shook his head. "No. Not really."

"What was he wearing?" She asked quietly.

"Jeans, boots, and a blue t-shirt." Mark chuckled.

"What?" Stopping the SUV, Abbi looked at him,

"He was also wearing that godawful yellow jacket you got him for his birthday." He flashed her an apologetic smile.

"He looks good in yellow. Besides, he likes it." She smiled at the memory of his excitement upon opening it. She raised a brow... In retrospect maybe he didn't like it so much, he'd been a little too excited over a jacket.

"Yeah... maybe," he agreed.

"He's quitting Mark..." Abbi said softly.

"Come again?" Mark frowned, looking at her. "What are you talking about, Abbi?"

"Ben told me he's done. He's quitting acting... retiring... is what he said."

"No way! He can't just quit!" Mark spat out. "Every director in the industry wants him. He can't just do that. Think of the money he will lose!"

Abbi inhaled deeply. She removed her foot from the brake, letting the SUV coast, and said, "Some things are more important than money. Besides, its his choice. I can't make that decision for him. He may change his mind. Speaking of which..." she paused. "Mark, he doesn't remember you or anyone else for that matter. Or that he's an actor. He only knows he is because the people that found him told him. All that he remembers is me..." She glanced at Mark. "He may never remember his past... And I'm not pressuring him to try."

Flabbergasted, Mark laid a hand on his chest and stared at her with a horrified expression on his face. "He doesn't remember me?" he asked in disbelief. "How could anyone not remember me?" He folded his arms across his chest and sulked. "I'm genuinely offended..."

"I'm sure it will come back to him... in time," Abbi muttered absently, scanning the ground ahead. They had to of reached a thousand feet by know. Abbi glanced down at the odometer and was shocked to see they had driven three miles. Looking up, she was just about to tell Mark when her eye caught something ahead. *What is that?*

She felt her heart quicken its beat. It looked like broken trees. Not like the crash site where it was a gradual breakage. But trees that were snapped off at the base as if a truck had barreled through them...

She hit the gas and sped up just a tiny bit. Her heart now felt like it would take flight as her eyes took in the scene. She pulled to a stop beside it. Hope flared in her chest.

"Mark, come on. I think it's Ben's seat!" She jumped out of the vehicle not waiting for him.

Abbi knelt beside the abandoned snow-covered seat placing a hand on it. She was staring at it. Picturing Ben strapped to it, unconscious. *Wait a minute... this may not be his.* But it *felt* like it was.

Tears sprang to her eyes as she glanced away, searching for anything that might belong to him.

Mark squatted, joining her finally. Nodding his head, he said, "Yup, that's his seat alright."

Moonlit Road

Abbi looked at him. "How can you be so certain?" she asked in a hushed voice.

"You see this?" He pointed to a bit of red sticking out of a crease in the seat. Tugging on it, he pulled it free. Flipping it between his fingers, he stared at it and said, "Ever since meeting you, every time he flies, Ben sticks this in the seat he sits in." He held it out for her to take.

"What does it say?" she asked.

"I have no idea Abbi. Ben never did say, and I never asked."

She was afraid to see what Ben wrote. She imagined him thinking it may be the last thing he'd ever be able to say to her, Abbi hesitated before taking it.

She did. Slowly she unfolded the paper and read the contents of the short note. She promptly covered her face with her hands and burst into tears. The paper slipped from her fingers, fluttering to the ground.

Mark glanced at it... *One moonlit night.* His brow creased in thought. What the hell... "What does that even mean Abbi?"

She wiped her eyes with her sleeves and leaned back on her heels. "Ahh God. It means it is his seat. He was here." She ran her hand over it, stroking it as if it were Ben. Trying desperately to swallow her tears, she continued, "He told me that he fell for me one moonlit night. The day we met," she said quietly, sniffling as the tears streamed down her face.

She took the note, carefully folded it and put it in her bra over her heart, for safekeeping. "Come on. We have to get back to the others." She hurriedly grabbed up anything she thought might belong to Ben. She didn't care if it was a button; she was taking it.

"You know what I don't get?" Mark asked.

"What's that?" Abbi answered, absently, her thoughts on Ben.

"How could he not remember me? I mean, if it wasn't for me selling him my house," he waved a hand in her direction, "he would never have met you."

Really? He's still going on about that. I should never have told him. She sighed heavily turning towards the SUV.

"I don't know Mark. The mind is a tricky thing. He didn't know me at first, either." Abbi glanced at him as she climbed behind the wheel, while Mark got in on the passenger side. "I'm sure it will all come back to him, it just takes time." *Now please drop it*. She thought as she started the engine and threw it into gear.

"Yeah. I guess you're right," he said looking out the window.

"Mark, you know Ben loves you." It was easy for her to say, she knew. If the tables were turned, she would be having a much worse time of it than Mark.

"Yeah, I know." He motioned out the windshield and nodded towards the five parked police cars. "Looks like the cavalry has arrived."

Abbi frowned. They were either there to help or they were there to arrest them. A car for each of them... She pulled the SUV to a stop and slowly got out.

"Abbi, Mark." Noah called them over. "This is my friend I was telling you about. Sheriff Jack Martin."

Jack touched the brim of his hat and nodded "Abbi, pleased to meet you." He stuck out his hand to Mark. "Mr. Donovan, I've heard a lot about you. I really admire your work."

Mark took the sheriff's hand in a firm grip. "Is that so? Call me Mark," he said. "So, what brings you all out here?" Mark asked gesturing to the cars.

"Um... Mark, hold that thought." Noah said as he passed by him to walk to Abbi's side.

"Abbi, Hun." Noah took her by the arm and guided her towards an officer.

"I want you to meet, Deputy Marleen Chesterton. She has some questions she needs to ask."

Moonlit Road

Abbi glanced at Noah then at Marleen. Something was up, and they didn't want her to know.

"Hi Abbi, how you are doing hunny?" Marleen smiled.

Abbi stared at her. Confidence oozed from every pore on her smiling face. Abbi wanted to dislike her for taking her away from what was going on. But try as she might, she couldn't, she felt drawn to her.

"I'm doing okay," Abbi sighed, tiredly.

"Oh, no you're not. Come here, girl." Marleen yanked open the front passenger door of her squad car. "You sit yourself down right there. Are you cold? Here let me get in the other side and I'll turn the heat on for you."

Abbi watched as she all but ran around the car to the driver side. "Wooeee, I gotta catch my breath! Here we go," Marleen said as she cranked the heat. She looked over to Abbi. Grabbing some-thing from the back seat, Marleen shoved a bag in front of Abbi's face. "Do you want a cookie, hunny?"

Abbi chuckled, pushing the bag away. "Ah, no thanks."

Selecting one from the bag Marleen asked, "You sure?" She stuffed one in her mouth. "They're chocolate mint."

Abbi held up a hand, "Positive. I'm good, thanks. What was it you wanted to ask me?" Abbi glanced at her.

"Oh, right!" Marleen reached into the glove box in front of Abbi. "Oops," she said, catching the handgun that slipped. "Don't want that shooting off in here, now do we?" she giggled.

Abbi's eyes grew large. *Was this lady for real?* "Nope, we don't want that to happen." She chuckled and shook her head.

"Here we are!" Marleen held up a book triumphantly.

The Jasper Killings... Right... She wants me to sign it...

"Would you mind?" Marleen raised hopeful eyes to her.

"Sure." Abbi felt her pockets. "Ah... I don't have a pen..."

Moonlit Road

"Here ya go." Marleen clicked the end of it and passed it to her. "You can sign it 'to my girlfriend Marleen'?" she asked, hopefully.

Why the hell not? "No problem." She signed the book and passed back the pen. Abbi held the book tightly to her chest. Something was bothering her; she just couldn't put her finger on it. Something about her book. She tried to remember it in detail. On any other given day, she could recite it word for word... well, mostly. But it was eluding her right now...

"Marleen. Do you think I could look at this for a minute?" Abbi squeezed the book tighter.

The look Marleen gave her made Abbi feel like she thought she was a fraud. Like she didn't really write it. *She likely thinks I'm some crazy lady who owns 20 cats...*

Holding the bag of cookies to her chest, Marleen stuffed another one in her mouth. Her eyes large in her round face. "Sure thing, hunny." She looked down at the bag she clutched to her chest. Slowly she tilted the bag towards Abbi. "You want a cookie now?"

Abbi burst out laughing, Marleen joined her. As tears sprang to their eyes, Abbi nodded. "Yes, I'll take a cookie now." She smiled her thanks. As she reached into the bag, they noticed the others looking at them as if they were nuts. Which promptly had them laughing hysterically again. It felt good to let off a little tension, even if was over something as silly as a damn cookie. That was until she saw the look on Mark's face...

Chapter 8

"Wait, what?" Mark raised his brows in outrage. "Whoa, whoa, whoa." He motioned for a timeout. "Let me get this straight..." He stood a moment, looking up at the trees as he rubbed his jaw. Finally, he looked at the sheriff. "What do you mean, they aren't agents?! Who the hell are they then?" he hissed.

"We aren't entirely sure." Jack said.

Mark stepped closer, raising his brows. Fearing that Abbi would overhear, in a hushed tone he questioned, "Hadn't you better find out?"

Noah put out a hand, urging Mark to stay put. "These things take time, Mark," he interjected. "We can't just go in there with guns blazing. Ben could be killed... if it's who we think it is."

"Yeah, well Abbi isn't going to wait. She'll flip." Mark said, looking worriedly at the squad car she was currently sitting in. The laughter coming from within carried to him and the officers. Mark saw the exact moment when she realized something was terribly wrong.

Mark nodded. Yes. Here it comes now. He watched as she came flying out of the car, rushing over to them as she stuffed something into her coat pocket.

"What?" she asked, tears already forming in her eyes.

She clenched her teeth, willing the cookie she just ate to stay down. Hoping beyond hope that she wouldn't lose it all over someone's shoes. "Someone better tell me what the hell is going on!"

"Uh." Noah cleared his throat. "Abbi," he wiped his mouth, "Ben was right. Those people aren't agents…"

She lowered her head and watched as the tip of her boot dug into the blackened earth. Tears spilled over her lashes, blinding her, yet she still gazed at the ground.

"Abbi, sweets. Are you okay?" Mark asked gently.

Her head bobbed up and down rapidly. She was going to lose it; she could feel it. Slowly she started to shake it from side to side as a low keening of agony escaped past her quivering lips.

"Come here, sweets." Mark enfolded her into his arms, holding her as she sobbed.

The one thing that kept her going was thinking that Ben was safe with the agents. How foolish she was. Abbi pulled away from Mark. She needed answers now.

"Sheriff, do you have any clue who they might be?" she asked, wiping her coat sleeve across her face. She noted the glance cross between Sheriff Martin and Noah, one she didn't like.

"Abbi…"

With one look Abbi effectively cut off Noah from finishing.

"Sheriff?" One brow arched in his direction; Abbi waited. The longer he took, the madder she got. "Are you going to answer my question?" she added testily.

"We aren't sure who they are…"

"Bullshit! You know very well who they are, so stop stalling and tell me."

Sheriff Jack Martin sighed. "I'm not at the liberty to discuss this with you, it's an open investigation."

Abbi smacked her thigh in frustration as looked around in wonder. "Right. An open investigation. I should have guessed," she jeered, looking at all of them. She whipped around, stalking towards the vehicle.

"Abbi, where are you going now?" Noah called.

"Back to the hotel. And if none of you want to walk, you best get in." She slammed the driver's door and revved the engine to life.

"Oh Lord, she's not kidding." Ava looked at Kim and Mark. All three scrambled to get to the SUV before she tore out of there.

"Noah, you better haul ass if you're coming with us," Mark called.

"I'm coming!" Noah yelled, hurtling over a fallen tree.

Abbi wasn't wasting any time. Noah was able to pull his feet in and slam the door, just in the nick of time before the SUV was thrown into reverse. Abbi spun the vehicle around and hit the gas.

"Jesus Abbi! Are you trying to scare the shit outta me?" Noah yelled.

Mark looked at him from the front seat as he once again gripped the bar.

"Buddy, you better hang on," he muttered, turning his head back to look out the windshield.

Breathing rapidly, Kim yelled, "Abbi for cripes sake slow down!" She hated going faster than a snail's pace. Kim covered her face when she saw that Abbi had no intention of stopping where the forest met the highway.

"Mom, you need to slow down, now!" Ava demanded, as the vehicle cranked a hard right, squealing onto the pavement.

Abbi had enough. She stomped on the brakes causing the vehicle to come to a screeching halt. She gripped the steering wheel.

Moonlit Road

Panting, she slowly turned in her seat and was met with four sets of terrified eyes staring at her. She wanted to scream at them all to shut the hell up but counted to ten instead.

"I'm sorry," she mumbled, mentally cursing at each one. "I…" she smoothed her hair down. "I had a moment. It won't happen again." She turned back in her seat and proceeded to drive south.

Noah gave Ava a look. Silently he mouthed to her 'where is she going?'

What in God's name is he saying? Ava frowned and squinted, shaking her head, silently conveying she didn't understand.

He leaned forward and did the same thing to Kim. She raised her brows and asked, "What the hell are you trying to say?"

Noah cleared his throat. "I said where is she going?"

The others remained silent, knowing now was not the time to ask Abbi anything.

Abbi raised her eyes to the rear-view mirror. She looked back at the road. *Where am I going?* The hotel was in the opposite direction. She had every intention of going that way, but something was tugging her south and damned if she would deny it.

She stuck her arm out in front of Mark. "Pull," she said, glancing at him. The look on his face, one would think she had thrown a slug at him.

"*What?*" he cried, shocked that she broke the silence.

She shook her arm. "My sleeve… pull on it will you? I'm hot."

Mark nodded. Not saying a word, he tugged on her sleeve as she pulled her arm free.

Abbi smiled her thanks.

"Do you want me to drive Abbi?" he quietly asked her.

"Nope." Was her quick response.

He looked out his window, watching… for what he didn't know. "Okay… it was just a thought." Mark glanced back at her. "Ah Abbi, sweets. Where *are* you going?"

"I'll know when we get there."

He let out a shaky laugh. "Of course, you will." He glanced at the others. "Why didn't we think of that?" he asked sarcastically, his laughter turning mechanical.

❧☙

The SUV ate mile after mile along the lonely paved road. The sun was rapidly making its decent on another day. Up ahead there was a town according to the road sign. Martinsville, population 5000. Abbi fleetingly wondered if it was named after the Sheriff's family. She didn't like Jack Martin. She had no clue as to why, but for some reason he rubbed her the wrong way. Maybe it was just that she was so damned tired. Tired of driving, tired of crying and especially tired of missing Ben.

Before she knew it the sun was down and tears still slipped down her cheeks as the streetlights streamed in the darkened car. She would never forgive herself if something happened to him. He was her light in a dark and cold world. Abbi felt a hand cover hers on the gearshift. She looked down to see Mark's hand on hers.

"Abbi. It's time we pulled over for the night, okay?" he asked her softly.

She pulled her hand away, and quickly swiped her cheeks. She nodded in agreement.

"Mom, there's a bed-and-breakfast." Ava pointed. "Why don't we stop there for the night," she suggested, the tiredness evident in her voice.

Moonlit Road

Abbi took a deep breath, wanting desperately to sound like she was in control. She failed miserably at it, "Sure, sounds great," she mumbled.

She signaled and pulled the SUV into the driveway. There before them stood an old Victorian home, something that looked like it could be home to a vampire.

"Um, guys… you sure about this?" Kim squeaked as she peered up at the house from her window.

"Hell yes!" Noah smacked his hands together. "Now this is the perfect spot for a movie, huh, Mark?"

Mark glanced out the window. "Sure… for a horror movie."

"I don't care if it's haunted. I'm so tired it won't make a bit of difference," Ava said.

"Nothing can be as scary as Abbi's driving." Kim grinned at her sister.

"You're alive, aren't you?" Abbi countered.

She loved her sister dearly, but watching the grin fall from Kim's face put a spring to Abbi's step.

"Come on. Let's check in." Ava said, pushing past everyone to walk up the steps.

Ava raised her hand just as the door sprung open. There before them stood a little old lady. A smile beaming on her wrinkled face.

Looking Abbi in the eye, she held out her hand and said, "Abbi… We have been expecting you all. Welcome to our humble abode. You all must be exhausted from that long drive. My name is Hester Riley."

All five of them looked from one to the other. The same question mirrored in their eyes… How did she know they had been driving for so long and how the hell did she know Abbi by name… and who was the 'we' that was expecting them?

Chapter 9

Ben could feel Abbi's warm breath on his face as he gazed into her eyes. God he would never tire looking into those orbs. She smiled at him then.

"I've missed you my love," he murmured as he tucked a silky strand of hair behind her ear. He tilted her chin upward with his finger and slowly bent to touch his lips to her soft mouth. The thrill had him groaning ... *with pain in his leg?*

Instantly awake, Ben bolted upright in bed. Grimacing as he glanced around searching for Abbi; he found himself alone in the darkened room. It was all just a dream.

His gaze darted to the door; the chair was still propped up under the knob, just as it had been every night since he had arrived in this hell hole.

Feeling defeated he searched the bed for his phone. He thumbed the power button on. He had sent Abbi a quick text telling her he was powering it off; he couldn't wait for a response. It was the only way to save what little battery life it had left. Thankfully, it held onto its charge. If he used it sparingly it might just last.

When was that again? A day ago, two? He waited for the home screen to load before checking to see when he sent it. Hoping she responded. The shrilling of a phone startled him, he fumbled with it, catching it just before it hit the floor. Flipping it over in his hand, he realized the ringing came from the other room. Holding his breath, he listened to see if anyone would answer. Sam's 'hello' came through the thin walls of the cabin.

Scooting to the edge of the bed, he silently grabbed the crutch from the floor.

Who would be calling her at 2:00 am?

He hobbled as quietly as he could to the door. Panting from the excursion, he placed his ear against it, straining to listen.

"Of course, boss…Yes, it was me that brought the plane down just as you requested."

What in the actual hell…?

Sam paused. Listening to the caller Ben imagined. Her next words had him cocking his head.

"Mr. Everett? Ah yes. The passenger name record indicated he was on the flight."

Who is she talking about? He moved his head and flattened his ear against the crack in the door. He dared not take a breath.

"No sir. There is no sign of him at this moment. After seeing the wreckage firsthand as you well know, I can guarantee he was killed in the crash, it likely will be weeks before his body is found… Why thank you sir! Yes, I'm sure the client will be thrilled as well…. I'm always available if you're needing… shall we say, 'another hit'."

Ben backed away in horror. He'd known something was off, but this? He slowly made his way back to the bed. He needed to think, to make sense of all this in his muddled mind. Something was way off. That was a definite, yes… he just couldn't put his finger on it.

Now what the hell am I going to do? Sam obviously is the 'hit-man'…does that mean Smitty is too? And who the bloody hell is Mr. Everett? He got up and stumbled to the window. He had to come up with a plan.

Glancing out the frosty edged pane of glass he saw that it had stopped snowing. The snow swirled along the ground, drifting here and there. Leaning on the sill, he looked out, searching for anything that could be a landmark he could tell Abbi about. There was nothing but the road and mile after mile of bare trees.

He thought he saw the twinkling of lights through the trees. If that was the case, maybe there was a house or a town nearby. He needed to get outside. The cabin was one floor so it wouldn't be that bad of a fall if he climbed out the window. Relief filled him as he looked at the ground. He could just crawl over the ledge and stand on the ground. Gripping the handles, he slowly raised it an inch. The cool breeze hit him like a blast from a freezer. *Wait... you need to tell Abbi first.*

He slowly closed the window. As much as he wanted to leave at that very moment, he knew if he took off now without anyone knowing he had left, he'd freeze to death before he was found.

He sighed heavily as he turned back to the bed and sat down. He had to figure this out. Rubbing his forehead in thought, he set out to do just that.

Why was Smitty so helpful if he was in on this? At least he acted helpful.

Something about this was all so damn familiar, he couldn't shake that feeling for the life of him. He laid back, willing his mind to remember what it was. Vague images as if he were walking in fog flashed through his mind. Frustration overtook him. It was no use, the harder he tried to remember the worse the pictures in his mind clouded over. He would need to relax. Not think so hard maybe.

A bang in the room next to his, startled him upright. Someone had flung the outside door open.

"Dean what the hell?" Sam hissed.

Does that woman not sleep?

It was a damn good thing he hadn't left. He never would have gotten far if he had. He was sure that man would love any excuse to put a bullet in his head.

"Where is he?" Dean slurred.

"Who? Smitty?" Sam questioned.

"Smitty's on watch." He yanked a chair out from the table and sat down. "No. Mr. Hollywood," came Deans sneer.

"You know full well I have to keep an eye on him. He's sleeping in the bedroom." Sam bristled. "Or he was until you came barging in…"

"I know what you're up to old woman…"

Old woman? Sam must be in character

"Is that so? And what might that be?"

By that time, Ben was back standing at the door. Carefully he eased the chair from under the doorknob. Despite her trying to kill him, he knew if things got ugly between the two, he would have to intervene. He reached for the doorknob and slowly turned it.

"You're trying to cash in on him. You're going to call the cops any day now and demand a ransom… I want in on it." Dean said with wickedness.

Ben's hand froze.

"Is that so? How much?" Sam questioned.

Piss on that… Ben grabbed the chair, stuck it back under the doorknob and made his way to the bed. *What the hell was I thinking…* he wondered sitting down.

For some reason he hadn't been. If someone had talked to Abbi like that, they would not be standing for long. But Sam wasn't Abbi. Not even close. He clearly didn't think, he just acted. A mistake he wouldn't make again.

Laying down on the bed, his thoughts turned to Abbi. Where they had been, since discovering his cellphone clenched tightly in his hand; strapped to a seat in the middle of the forest.

His phone lit up the room. Picking it up, he hit the text notification. His face softened when he saw her name.

Moonlit Road

'I know you're likely sleeping Ben, but it eludes me. You probably won't get this till after we find you, but I had to tell you. We found where your seat landed... and I have your note. I never told you this, but I fell in love with you the same moonlit night on my front porch. I never wanted to let you go and I still don't. I just thought you should know that. Love Abbi'

He wanted so badly to respond. But he couldn't. He knew if he did, what little charge he had left would quickly be depleted. He pressed the power button, as one single tear ran down his cheek...

Ben awoke to sunlight streaming through the window and a dire need to use the bathroom. Feeling as weak as a newborn, he struggled to sit up. Leaning over the edge of the bed, he picked up his crutches and moved to stand. A wave of dizziness had him almost toppling backwards onto the bed. He had to get out of there, today. He didn't care if he died trying. It would be better than being locked up in this hell hole a minute longer.

He'd already worked out the plan in his head. He would go out to the other room where Sam aka Daisy would be, having her morning coffee and smoke. They would make small talk like they did for the past few days, and then she would leave to go work at the farm across the yard. He would be left alone for the next few hours until someone came to check on him. That time in between is when he would make his escape. But first, he would let Abbi know his intentions. Hopefully, she would get to him in time. Before someone showed up, likely Smitty.

Now there was something about Smitty that just was not adding up. He wasn't cold like Sam. To put it bluntly she was a certified bitch. Smitty genuinely seemed concerned about him. Bringing him food and pain meds, along with the daily newspaper. No, Smitty wasn't anything like the others.

Ben made his way to the door. He removed the chair, like he did every morning since getting there from underneath the doorknob. Opening the door, he mumbled a "Good morning" as he headed to the bathroom.

He was washing his hands when he happened to look at his reflection in the mirror above the sink. He stopped. Staring at the stranger before him. He was stunned, realizing he hadn't seen his reflection since the accident. He must have lost weight as his eyes seemed sunken. He looked down at his clothes. They were a bit loose, he noticed, and stained, wreaking of sweat and blood. He glanced back up at the mirror. A beard hid the gauntness of his face and the pallid skin beneath. He was confident that he'd never had a beard in his life. Judging from the photos on his phone at least. Either way, it would have to go, it itched like he had been bitten by fleas. Which would not surprise him any if that were the case, considering his current living conditions.

He opened the cabinet, looking for a pair of scissors and razor, he heard the outside door slam shut followed by footsteps across the wood plank floor. The sound of a chair being dragged from under the table, told Ben exactly who it was. Dean…

The beard would have to wait. Ben reached out grabbing the doorknob. Taking a steadying breath, he pulled the door open. The two sitting at the table watched as he made his way over. He pulled out a chair and sat down hard.

Glancing towards Sam he saw her in character as Daisy. It was on the tip of his tongue to comment on that fact in front of Dean but thought better of it. Who knows what shit storm that would create? Instead he turned and stared at Dean. The hatred for the man evident in his gaze.

"What's your problem?" Dean sneered.

Ben squinted.

"I'll tell you what my problem is. Or how about you give me a baseball bat and let me smash your leg with it and maybe then you'll see what my problem is, hmm?"

Dean snickered in response." He pointed at Ben "I like you. "It just so happens today is your lucky day I'd say," he crooned.

Moonlit Road

At Daisy's questioning look, Dean sent her conspiratorial wink.

"You get to meet the boss man of this here operation. He'll decide your fate."

Daisy made a sound in her throat.

Dean sent her a warning look. "Hush old woman. The boss requested an audience with Mr. Hollywood." He pushed away from the table and came around to Ben. "Come on. It's showtime. Move it, let's go."

Ben got up from the table. *Well, there goes my plans of escaping... for now.*

He followed Dean from the cabin with Daisy, shuffling along to bring up the rear. Ben had to give her credit; she was a pretty convincing actress... *Actress? Hmm. Now that makes sense...*

Brightness from the sun assaulted Ben's eyes causing him to fumble on a rock. Dean caught him just in time before he fell to the ground. In a low whisper, that only Ben could possibly hear, Dean said, "It's okay buddy. I got you."

Ben stared at him in shock. What happened to the badass from moments before? He had to be imagining it.

Dean boomed, "This way lady and gent." As he opened the door to the farm. The smell of skunk once again hit Ben full force.

Knowing he couldn't possibly be high from the plants; something was making him feel sick. He swallowed trying to stop the nauseous bile from surging up his throat. Yes. The scent was over-whelming. But Ben was sure it was the fact that a bullet could find its way into his spine at any moment. In his weakened state he would be a prime target for anyone who chose to do a little practice shooting.

The trio trudged on. Towards, the back of the building, Dean led them to a door. Pushing it open, he stepped aside allowing Ben, followed by Daisy, to enter first.

Moonlit Road

Ben glanced around the room; his eyes fell immediately on the man standing against the wall. Smitty. He looked as if he was the one that was facing the firing squad.

The room smelled of stale cigar smoke and brandy. Two plush leather chairs in front of a large mahogany desk, sat in front of a bay window that overlooked a river. The chair slowly swiveled around. Ben felt immediate relief when he saw who the man was sitting behind the desk.

...Dean called him the boss man... This just keeps getting better and better...

The man leaned forward and offered his hand to shake.

"Well hello Mr. Everett. It's nice to finally meet you. Take a load off." He gestured to one of the chairs.

Ben ignored the proffered hand and sat.

Everett? There's that name again... Other than being called by a different name, the only thing running through his mind was how doomed he was.

Chapter 10

"Okay then." Sheriff Jack Martin said, leaning back in his chair. He picked up a sheet of paper that was laying on his desk. Scanning it, his brows drew together in a frown. He laid the paper back down and folded his hands in front of him.

Ben Everett had quite the lengthy career record.

Jack glanced at him sitting there across the desk. His clothes were dirty and disheveled. The smell of his stench reached his nostrils clear across the desk. Jack Martin wrinkled his nose in dis-taste. He wondered what the big shot actor thought about his cur-rent predicament.

"So, Ben. You don't mind me calling you by your given name now do you son?"

"Would it matter. No?" Ben shook his head. "I didn't think so."

Jack nodded. He pointed to the paper on his desk. "I got my boys to do a little digging. Seeing how in these parts, most have never heard of you. You're quite the star, aren't you?"

Ben couldn't confirm nor deny what he said. That part of his memory was still missing, he shrugged his shoulders in way of an answer.

"It also says that you are living in Canada with Abbi Petersen. Now, that name folks around here know of. I already knew that, having the pleasure of meeting the little hell cat myself," He said, a lecherous smile spread on his fat greasy lips.

At the mention of Abbi's name, a steely cold went through Ben's veins. *What the hell is he insinuating?*

Ben took a deep breath, his nostrils flared. He looked at the Sheriff, giving him a deadpan stare. "Do you have a point to all this interrogation sheriff?" He asked.

"I do. I think we will keep you just a bit longer. I'll give Abbi a call. Anonymously of course. Telling her that if she wants to see you alive again, she'll pay up. Perhaps…in more ways than one."

Ben gripped the arms of his chair. He had to resist the urge to beat the smile off that fat smug face. He wasn't surprised in the least to hear about a ransom. How many times was that now? Too many to count. But for him to talk about Abbi like that was more than he could handle. He *had* to restrain himself, and the sooner he got out of there the better. Without a doubt, Ben knew the hired thugs would be all over him if the Sheriff so much as squeaked.

Ben sent the man a murderous stare, "Are we through here?" he asked, every word dripping with malice. That was all he had to say to see the instant fear spring to the Sheriffs face.

Jack nodded rapidly, "Certainly. You can go back to the cabin now."

Satisfied, Ben inclined his head as if he were dismissing the man.

Heaving himself up from the chair, he slowly made his way to the door. Turning back, he gave one last long look before exiting. Stepping out into the hall with Daisy and Smitty right behind him, he heard the Sheriff talking to Dean. His words almost caused Ben to falter, but he refused to show any emotion.

Once I get back to the cabin, it's time to come up with a new escape plan.

It was either that or come dawn, Dean was ordered to send him to his maker…

"I'll take him back to the cabin Daisy." Smitty said, as they turned down the hallway that lead to the clinic and the door to outside.

"Sure, I have some paperwork to go over." She sounded relieved, as she scurried towards her office.

"Come on Ben, I'll get you something to eat." Smitty held the door for him to cross the threshold to outside.

The sun was no longer blinding as clouds gathered in the sky. It had the look and feel of snow in the air. Ben didn't care, he was leaving tonight one way or another.

Neither man said a word, both lost in their own thought as they made their way to the cabin.

Smitty hurried ahead to open the cabin door for Ben. Once inside, Ben went right to the table and collapsed on the closest chair.

"What do you feel like eating?" Smitty asked.

Ben sighed, all he wanted to do was sleep right in the chair. He didn't even have the energy to fall into the bed. "Nothing, I'm not hungry."

Smitty opened the fridge and took out a carton of eggs. Slapping a frying pan on the stove he turned the element on high and quickly cracked six eggs in the sizzling pan. Whipping them with a fork he said, "You need to eat, you have to keep your strength up."

Ben wasn't giving his intentions away. There was no way he would even hint that he was planning an escape.

"For what, just to be killed at dawn?" He spat out.

Smitty turned from the stove to look at him.

"Were you not listening the first night you came here?" Smitty asked.

Ben squinted in thought and shook his head. His stomach growled at the smell coming from the stove. He leaned back in his chair trying to appear relaxed and laid his hands on the rumbling, hoping to silence it.

Here it is the part about him being with the DEA...

"Right..." Ben nodded, "You and Sam being agents." He folded his arms across his chest. He didn't buy their story then and he wasn't now. Sam made it perfectly clear what kind of agent she was.

Smitty turned the stove off and dumped the eggs onto a plate. Sitting it before Ben he said, "Yeah that's it. I talked to my superior and I was given the order to take you out."

"Come again?" Ben asked.

Just how many people have it in for me?

"Hell. No! I didn't mean 'take you out' as in shoot to kill. I meant remove you from here!"

Ben let his guard down, just a bit. A tiny sliver of hope flared in his chest.

"When?" He asked, picking up the fork he dug into the eggs.

Smitty brought two cups of steaming coffee to the table. Sitting down, he leaned towards Ben.

"Tonight, after 4 am." Smitty pointed to the plate. "You might want to slow down on that just a bit. You might get sick."

Ben's hand froze midway to his gaping mouth. He looked down at the eggs.

Did Smitty poison them? No. I got to trust someone.

Shrugging, he stuck the fork in his mouth and looked at Smitty. "Why so late?"

If this fails, at dawn I'm a goner.

"Dean is on the night watch tonight. He always falls asleep around 3:30. By 4 am he will well off to lala land."

Ben nodded. Stuffing the last of the eggs in his mouth, he savored the last bite.

"So. What's the plan?" he asked, pushing his plate away.

"The plan is simple. You crawl out of your window at exactly 4: am. I'll keep watch from across the clearing. Just to make sure you're not spotted. Sit tight for a minute. If it's all clear, I'll send out three sharp whistles. There will be a van waiting down the road a bit. You will have to walk though. Do you think you can manage?"

Ben nodded. If it meant getting out of this hell hole and back to Abbi, he'd crawl if he had to.

"Good, you better get some rest." Smitty looked at his watch. "You have 16 hours."

Ben chuckled, "I'm sure I'll be well rested by then." He frowned. Should he mention what he'd overheard Sam and Dean talking about the other night?

Thinking it for the best he took a deep breath. "Ah, can I mention one thing that's been bugging me?"

"Shoot."

"The other night Dean came bursting in at around 2 am. He said he knew what Sam was up to. Though he called her Daisy." Ben looked at Smitty for a reaction. There was none.

"Yeah? Well he only knows her as Daisy. Go on."

"He wanted to split on the ransom he knew she was going to ask for me. If she's an agent, she's a dirty one."

Smitty nodded. "I had my doubts about her too." He took a sip of his coffee. "We arrived together, as joint investigators. I immediately felt something off and so I contacted my superior over it. There is an 'agent' Sam Perkins and by that, I mean her undercover name. We never use our real names when undercover." He paused. He had the look of a person that had given too much information out. He shrugged and continued. "I can't vouch for her as a person. Being from different agencies, I never knew her before. I shouldn't have told you all of that, but I'm trying to be as transparent as much as possible."

Moonlit Road

Ben nodded. "I really appreciate it mate." He frowned. Something was still bothering him, and he had to ask. "So how long have you two been here?"

"Four months, one month longer than Dean."

"Dean? I thought he would have been here longer, given his role. He's what? The manager?" Ben asked nonchalantly.

Smitty chuckled. "He likes to think he is. I had him checked out too. He has a record longer than your arm."

Ben nodded and scratched his beard. "Bloody hell, this thing is driving me nuts."

"Hey. Do you want a shower? I can get you a razor and a change of clothes?"

"I would give up my left nut for one." Ben laughed.

"No need for that." Smitty raised his hand and got up from the table. "I'll be right back. If you want, get in now and I'll leave everything on that table there by the bathroom." He walked to the door and stopped. Turning around to look at Ben, Smitty said "I know this really isn't the time to ask. But when this is all said and done, can I get your autograph?"

Ben smiled, genuinely for the first time in what felt like months.

"I'll do one better than that. If you get me out of here alive and back to Abbi in one piece, I'll fly you up to Canada for a week."

"Right on!" Smitty laughed, as he headed out the door.

༄༅༄

Ben laid staring at the ceiling. Darkness had fallen some time ago judging by the light of the full moon. He had no idea what the time was, but it felt like it was past midnight. Surprisingly, he had slept most of the day. A good solid eight hours, or at least his body felt like he had. He hadn't felt this energized in God knew how long. A hot shower and a shave would do that to anyone. But that wasn't it. He knew it was the thought of seeing Abbi again that had him feeling this way.

Despite being well rested, he felt himself drifting off to sleep again. That was until he heard Abbi crying the name Franklin in his ear. He bolted upright in bed. His eyes immediate were drawn to a faint, misty apparition in the corner by the door. He rubbed his eyes, sure that what he was witnessing was nothing more than the light of the moon shining through the trees. It wasn't...it was still there.

Who or what is this?

A young man stared at him from the corner. Dressed in an old army uniform, he floated towards the bed in a misty haze. Coming to a standstill beside it, he pointed towards the window.

Ben heard the man's voice, not out loud, but in his mind, telling him it was time to go.

Within a second the figure of the young man disappeared into a misty haze as it passed through the glass pane of the window.

He shook his head. God, he needed a splash of cold water on his face. He was trying to convince himself that what he saw was not real.

It was just a dream Ben. Nothing more than a dream...But if it really was a dream...why am I sitting up wide awake?

Trying to put it all behind him, he felt for his phone. Without picking it up he pressed the power button. He needed to know the time.

Surprised at how chilly the room was he grabbed his coat from the foot of the bed and tugged it on. Picking up his phone he turned it over. The display lit up the room, a chill ran up his spine... it was 3:55 am. He had five minutes before he was to climb out the window.

Seeing he had a missed text from Abbi he quickly opened it. A soft smile came to his lips. A simple 'Hi' was all it said. Man,

Moonlit Road

he loved her. He started to send her a reply letting her know what was going on, on second thought, he would send it to all the people she had mentioned before. Adding Mark, Ava and Kim from his contacts to the message, his thumb paused over the send button. *No... I better wait.* He didn't want to jump the gun in case he never made it outside. He didn't want Abbi anywhere near here if it could be helped. Especially if he got caught.

The battery, with any luck with hold its charge. At twenty percent, he was confident he would be able to send it later. Lucky for him, he'd been able to sneak using Daisy's charging cord when she was gone.

He saved it as a draft and shoved it in his pocket. As soon as he was outside, he would send it. Taking a deep breath, he gripped the handles on the window sash. Slowly inch by inch he raised it. Unexpectedly a loud creak echoed in the room.

"Sonofabitch!" he muttered softly. Why hadn't he thought to open it when he was alone in the cabin?

Holding his breath, he waited for the telltale footsteps that would tell him that someone heard. Nothing. He shoved it open, a blast of cold air rushed in, almost taking his breath away. Leaning out he looked around. There was a corner to the right of the window that was in shadows. The perfect spot to wait.

Now how the hell am I going to do this? He looked down at the crutches.

Deciding the best option was to put one crutch out the window followed by his good leg. He set out to do just that.

Slowly he maneuvered outside. Panting, from the exertion, he leaned back in the corner and glanced around. Satisfied he was alone he took his phone from his pocket. Looking down, he hit the send button on the message just as he heard the unmistakable slide of a 40 caliber semi-automatic being cocked.

"Did you honestly think I was going to let you get away?" Daisy asked. She motioned with the gun. "Come on, move it."

Where the hell is Smitty?

Moonlit Road

Feeling defeated, Ben slowly moved from the corner. Rounding the side of the cabin he headed towards the front. The sound of a shotgun being cocked echoed in the stillness.

"Not so fast there, little lady." Came the unmistakable sneer.

Ben stopped and turned around. Dean stood, pointing a gun at Daisy's head.

Bloody hell! This just keeps getting better and better…

Chapter 11

Abbi was laying on an ancient settee in the sitting room of the old B&B. She could already feel the kink starting in her neck as her head leaned uncomfortably on the wooden arm. She had to get up but couldn't bring herself to move.

She waited, phone in hand, willing Ben to respond. It was silly she knew, but she had just sent him a text; a simple 'Hi'. He never did respond to her last one, the one telling him when she fell in love with him. She doubted he would be up at 3:30 am, yet she remained still.

A few minutes longer wouldn't hurt. She was foolish she knew. Days ago, he'd told her his phone was dying. There was no way it could hold its charge.

Mark was prattling on about the injustices of the world. She had long ago stopped listening to him. Sitting before the cozy fireplace in Hester Riley's parlor, they had been discussing how strange it was that they hadn't been kept in the loop to the progress of the investigation. What was even stranger, was the fact that everyone seemed to stop talking about the plane crash and the fact that Ben was still missing.

"Abbi? … Abbi, are you asleep?" Mike asked in a loud whisper.

She looked at him. "No." was her simple response.

He raised his brows in question. "Did you not hear a word I said?"

Moonlit Road

"Ah... Nope?" At his frown, she felt the need to apologize. "I'm sorry Mark, my mind is not in the present. It has nothing to do with you, I promise. It's just..."

"Ben. I know, I get it." he returned.

"Yeah." she replied softly. A sudden overwhelming sadness overcame her. One that she wondered if it would ever go away. Shaking her head to focus on the moment at hand, she said, "What was it you were saying?"

"Oh nothing."

Nodding, she glanced back down at her phone.

"I just wondered what it was you stuffed in your pocket."

She gave him a puzzled look. "What? When?" she wrinkled her brow trying to remember.

"The other day when you came flying out of the cop's cruiser."

She slowly sat up. She had no recollection of it. *What was it she had stuffed in there?*

"Where is my coat?" She asked, setting her cell on the coffee table, she quickly got up off the settee.

"Ava hung it on the coat tree in the foyer." Mark nodded towards the general direction of it.

He watched as she sailed out of the room, minutes later she came back with the coat in her hands. She pulled the pockets out. A balled-up tissue, some loose change and a gum wrapper, spilled onto the coffee table beside her cell phone.

Mark shook his head as he looked at the table. "Nope, none of that. It was something fairly large," he said, spreading his hands apart.

"Which pocket was it?" Abbi looked at him for the answer.

"The right one, Abbi. I watched you put it in when you flew out of the car."

Moonlit Road

She fumbled, turning the coat to face her. Sticking her hand in she pulled out a copy of the Jasper Killings.

Her book! Now she remembered. She'd asked Marleen if she could look at it. She must have absently stuck in in her pocket in her hurried state.

"Huh." Mark said. "Do you always carry that around?"

"Of course not. Its Marleen's." Abbi explained, glancing at him she noticed the confusion on his face.

"The cop. You know, the female one who had me sit in her car while you were talking to the sheriff and Noah."

"Oh, that's right! Why do you have it?"

"I asked her if I could look at it for a minute," She said, sitting down she hugged it to her chest.

"…Why? You wrote it." He said, as if she needed reminding.

Abbi flipped through the pages, she was in the middle of searching for something, she wasn't sure what it was.

"I'll know when I find it…" she said absently.

With a worried look on his face Mark's eyes grew large as he nodded, "Rigghht."

He got up and laid a hand on her shoulder. "I'm going to bed Abbi. Don't stay up too late…" he gave her a brotherly kiss on the top of her head and walked towards the stairs. Stopping at the archway, he paused and looked back at her.

He was worried of the uncertainty of Ben's disappearance, but he was also worried about Abbi. Not only was his best friend missing but he was afraid Abbi was losing her mind. He just wasn't sure which was worse…

Abbi suddenly felt cold. She put her coat on and stuffed her belongings, where they belonged, in her coat pockets. She checked her cell to see if Ben had replied, it was 3:46 am. Disappointed that he hadn't responded, she dropped it in her pocket too. Sitting on the edge of the settee, she opened her book and scanned through the chapters.

"Here it is." She mumbled to herself.

Detective Ethan Fields surveyed the scene before him. The day that changed hundreds of lives forever. This was no 'accident'. No. This was a crime. A cold-hearted, premeditated crime.

Passenger trains did not just blow up while travelling on the rails across the countryside. Ethan glanced around. And they sure as hell didn't blow asteroid sized holes in the ground either.

The gaping hole in the earth only confirmed his suspicions. No. Someone was after Kingston Parker the Third. Heir to a mighty fortune…in paper products of all things. He was to be on that train. There was no way that someone would wake up one morning and decide today was the day. The day to blow up a train full of strangers. But who would do such a thing, Ethan wondered?

The most logical place to look first was the family. But Kingston Parker was the only living heir and the last in his family lineage. No, it had to be someone with a grudge…

Abbi snapped the book shut. She leaned back, slowly exhaling, staring off into space.

Was there a connection? Was all this planned based on my book?

A cough beside her interrupted her musings, startling her so, that she just about jumped out of her skin. Scanning the chapters of the book, she had been so engrossed in what she was reading, that she had failed to see the frail old lady sitting in the chair Mark had vacated minutes before.

"Jesus, Mary and Joseph! Where the heck did you come from? You scared the crap out of me!" She exclaimed breathlessly.

"I'm sorry dear. I saw you with your nose in that book." Hester looked at it pointedly. "I didn't want to scare you. I see that didn't work out so well now did it."

Abbi pushed her hair back from her face and noted the sadness on Hester's face. "It's okay. I'm just a bit jumpy. Lack of sleep will do that I guess..." she smiled. "Was there something you needed?"

"I've been so busy; I haven't had a chance to sit down with you and talk... To tell you, that I know why you're all here." Hester said, a soft smile on her lips.

A foreboding feeling suddenly ran over Abbi's body. Maybe it was just the house. It reminded her of a vampire's lair, or maybe it was something more...

"What do you mean Hester. I... I'm not following you." Abbi stammered.

"Do you mind if I tell you a story Abbi?"

Shaking her head Abbi replied, "Of course not. Please do."

"Well, it was an awfully long time ago. I was about your age; just a young woman."

Abbi's brows rose in surprise. *How old is she is she thinks I'm young?*

"I was in love with a man. My goodness he was beautiful." A wistful smile crossed Hester's wrinkled face. "You see, he was sent to Germany to fight the war. I was so lost. Beside myself really." Melancholy flashed across her face as she looked down at her hands, her memories taking her back in time. "There was a scrimmage that his platoon was involved in. All of them perished that fateful day." A tear streaked down her soft cheek.

"Oh, my goodness!" Abbi reached out, laying her hand over Hester's. "I'm so sorry to hear that."

Hester looked at Abbi, without batting an eyelash, she said, "Oh don't be dear! I thought I would never see him again, but he came back to me. You see, he's still here." Hester glanced around the room, her eyes settling on the spot beside her. "He's sitting right next to me."

Whaaat? Abbi had always believed in the idea of spirits walking the earth, especially ones taken so suddenly. But to hear that... *oh hell no!!*

Abbi snatched her hand away as if she were burned by an invisible flame.

Hester leaned forward, in a hushed tone she said, "My Franklin told me you were coming here. And why..."

Okay, I've lost it... She did not just imply there was a ghost sit-ting beside her, did she?

Abbi giggled nervously. "Oh right! Well..." She nodded, feigning a yawn, she let out a big stretch.... *The lady is off her rocker.*

"Um it was nice chatting with you Hester, but I think it's time I went to bed."

Not wanting it to appear that she was attempting a hasty retreat. She slowly got up and walked towards the archway.

Hester turned watching her walk away. "Abbi... one more thing dear."

Abbi stopped, frozen to the spot. She dared not turn around for fear of seeing Franklin sitting beside the old woman.

"My Franklin told me to tell you. Ten miles to the east, then turn right. In the middle of... Slow down Franklin...!"

A tingling sensation skittered up Abbi's back, the hair on her neck rising as the seconds ticked by. She could feel the goosebumps dimple on her skin as if something were hovering behind her.

"Yes, yes I'll tell her! Abbi dear, he said, ten miles to the east, then turn right. It will take you to the middle of Sterling forest. A lonely dirt trail passes through it called..." Hester paused as if waiting for something. Nodding she said, "Moonlit Road is what it's called. It winds along and ends at a long white building."

Moonlit Road

Ben told me it was a dirt road and a white building... It can't be... Abbi slowly turned around. Hester was looking not at Abbi but into space. The space Abbi had just left.

"He said it smells of skunk. Skunks? Why in heavens name would it smell like skunks?" Hester asked the empty air to her right.

Oh my God!! Tears streamed down Abbi's cheeks. *It just can't be...*

Hester looked at her now, a worried look on her features. "Oh dear…"

"*What?!?* What did Franklin *say?*" Abbi cried in a panic. She knew she was going nuts, wanting answers from a 'ghost'. The room was spinning, she felt like she was in a vortex and she didn't care. She had to know what Franklin was saying.

"He said you will find who you're missing, there." Hester sighed, "You need to slow down Franklin." She looked to Abbi. "I'm sorry. He has so much to say he isn't making sense." Hester looked to the air at her right again. "Yes, yes. I'll tell her. He said one moonlit night is all it took?"

Oh Lord...How does she know? Mark. Mark, he must have said something.

"He also said to tell you, all you want for Christmas is Ben?" Hester squinted and shrugged her frail shoulders, "Does that mean something to you?"

Abbi could feel the blood drain from her face as her knees buckled under her.

"Oh my! You need to hurry, Abbi. Ben doesn't have much time…"

Abbi had three choices. She could faint, she could scream and run through the house or she could drive as fast as she could east and find that lonely dirt trail called Moonlit Road.

Quickly, she closed the distance between them. Abbi bent down, wrapping her arms around Hester's frail shoulders, she hugged her and said, "Thank you Hester, and please tell Franklin, I thank him eternally for all his help."

She quickly turned and ran up the stairs to wake the others. *Do I dare believe the ramblings of a lonely old woman? Your damned right I do!*

To her knowledge, not one of them had mentioned Ben. And if they had, Ben and she were the only two who knew what she wanted for Christmas…

Chapter 12

The vehicle was flying down the road with Abbi at the wheel, in the dead of the night. Once again, all five of them were loaded into the SUV, headed on a wild goose chase.

After running up the stairs of Hester's home, Abbi quickly shook everyone awake, telling them they had to go now. The only way to get them motivated was to tell them she wasn't coming back. In less than five minutes they were all piling into the vehicle.

"Where in hell are we going now, Abbi?" Kim yawned tiredly from the passenger seat. "And will you put your damn window up?!"

"Sorry, if I close it, I'll miss the turnoff." Abbi muttered, more to herself than to anyone else.

Mark, Ava and Noah where all huddled together for warmth in the back seat. Mark leaned close to Ava, his mouth mere inches from her ear.

"If we don't find Ben soon, you do realize we are going to have to take drastic measures, right?"

Ava nodded in silent agreement. She was in denial that her mother was losing it. But her mom's actions were now speaking louder than any words ever could. Her mother would likely disown her, Ava knew that. But Abbi was leaving them little choice…

"There!! Kim, what does that road sign say?" Abbi pointed excitedly, pulling the vehicle to a stop.

The logical thing to do would have been to drive along side of the sign, but no one was logical at that moment in time. "It's too dark to see," Kim reached for the door handle, shoving the door open, she said, "Hang on a second."

Ambling over to the post, Kim stopped, and looked up at the sign. She swung her head back towards the vehicle, shouted something and motioned to the sky, then pointed to the road.

"What in the hell is she doing?" Noah questioned from the backseat.

"Ah...I don't know," Ava said, leaning forward watching Kim.

Mark opened his window and yelled, "This isn't the time for charades, Kim!"

Abbi glanced at the clock on the display. 4:03 am. They had to hurry. She stepped on the gas and steered towards Kim. "What did it say?" she asked, pulling aside Kim.

"I was trying to tell you its called Moonlit Road...I thought one of you would have figured out the reference of me pointing to the moon and the road," she huffed, slamming the door closed.

Abbi didn't move. Franklin had said Moonlit Road, the only problem with that was he didn't say which way...left or right.

She threw the gearshift into park. Turning in her seat she looked at all of them one by one.

"Guys I have something to tell you... you're likely going to think I'm crazy. And I don't blame you if you do." She paused wondering how she would put it in a way that sounded less absurd.

"I...Hester and I had a talk tonight. She told me a story. How she had been in love with a man that was called to war." She took a deep breath. "Um, he died. Over in Germany I think she said. Anyway, he came back to her..." Abbi put a hand to her head.

My God this even sounds crazy to me!

She giggled then, almost uncontrollably. "He still lives there... err... well he's there with her. Anyhow, he told her to tell me where to find Ben." She looked at each one, rushing on she added, "And so here we are."

They all had 'the look'. The look of how they could have her committed without her knowledge.

"I know what you're thinking. I'm crazy, right? I swear on Ben's life I'm not. Franklin told her things that she couldn't possibly have known."

Kim broke the silence first. "Franklin? Who is Franklin?"

"Franklin is Hester's love... *Wait!*" Mark answered. "No this is *wrong!* Abbi sweets, I know more than anyone else what you're going through right now. But you have to stop this!" he reasoned.

Abbi's throat stung. Try as she might to fight it, her eyes filled, the tears slipping down her cheeks in rivers. She had been fighting so desperately to not cry, but having Mark doubt her of all people, was more than she could take.

Her lips quivered. "Mark, you have no idea what I've gone through, what I'm going through every day since Ben has been gone." She felt like screaming her lungs out but didn't have the energy to do so. She pointed a finger at him, jabbing the air. "Don't you *dare* sit there and tell me that you do." Her voice broke on a sob as her gaze raked over each one of them. "*None* of you know what I am going through, and I pray to God you never do."

She turned back and laid her forehead on the steering wheel. Silent sobs wracked her body. She shouldn't have said that to Mark. He was only trying to help. But he didn't believe her, none of them did.

Ava reached out a hand, rubbing Abbi's back she said, "Mom? What did Franklin tell Hester?"

Without moving, Abbi took a steadying breath. Sniffling she said, "He told her to tell me to go ten miles to the east, then turn right. It will take you to the middle of Sterling forest, he said."

Everyone in the vehicle but Abbi looked out the windows…

They were in the middle of a forest.

"There was a sign when we turned on this road that said Sterling Forest," Kim said in a hushed tone.

"Yes. And a lonely dirt trail passes through it called…" Abbi squeezed her eyes shut. "Moonlit road. It will wind along to a white building. That smells of skunks…"

"Skunks!" Ava muttered.

"Pot plants I bet." Noah stated.

"Yeah. Ben told me it was filled with marijuana. They call it *The Farm*." Abbi said leaning back in her seat. She looked up, trancelike, she continued. "Franklin told Hester that I'll find who I'm missing there."

She turned to look at Mark. Raising her brows, she said, "He told Hester what Ben wrote on that note."

"How?!" he asked, a puzzled look on his face.

Abbi sighed and shrugged her shoulders, "I thought maybe you mentioned it."

"I swear Abbi, I didn't breathe a word of it to anyone."

She was back in her trance… staring through Mark she said, "He knew what I wanted for Christmas..."

"Which is…?" Kim asked.

Before Abbi could answer, all their cell phones went off at once.

Everyone, except Noah searched their pockets. As one, they all said the same thing… "Ben…?"

"Bingo…" Was all Abbi had to say. Going with her gut instinct. She cranked the steering wheel left and gunned the engine.

"Someone quick. Read me that text please?" She asked.

"I'm so sorry Abbi for ever doubting you." Mark blubbered from the back.

"It's okay. I would've doubted me too if I were you." She replied.

Abbi took her eyes off the road for a second to look at her sister. "Kim?"

"Yeah Abbi?"

Nodding towards the cell phone in Kim's hand she asked, "Can you read me that text?"

"Oh! Right. Sure thing." Kim looked down at her phone and cleared her throat. "'*Hi back at you love.*'" Kim felt tears come to her eyes. Waving a hand in front of her face she said, "Ava, you read it."

Abbi looked in the rear-view mirror. Ava's face too was wet with tears.

What in the world did Ben say? I should have read it myself…

Seeing how Ava would be no help, Abbi determined Mark wouldn't be either. Every so often she could hear a sniff coming from his direction.

"Ava, honey, give Noah your phone to read." She gently said. "Noah, would you?".

"Sure, I'll do that." he said taking the phone from Ava.

"Okay, here goes. '*Hi back at you love. I'm letting you know that I will be leaving here tonight. I need to. I just had to let you know that you may get a call from the 'boss man'. They are going to demand a ransom from you...'* Abbi, I think you need to pull over." Noah said quietly.

There was no way she was pulling over, the road was just starting to wind, any minute the white building would come into view.

She shook her head, "No. Keep talking Noah."

He sighed, "Alright than... *'Don't pay it Abbi. They have every intention of killing me at dawn'.*"

Abbi's foot slipped off the gas pedal.

Heaven help me, maybe I should pull over.

No! You need to keep going Abbi...

"Sorry," she mumbled. Stepping on the gas even more.

Noah continued, "*'I should mention who the 'boss man' is. He's a cop. A Sheriff. Jack Martin. Do NOT trust him Abbi'...* Holy Shit!" Noah shouted. "I trusted that dude."

Let me see that, Mark grabbed the cell out of Noah's hand, and picked up where Noah had ended "'*I have some help from Smitty/Calvin. I know what you're thinking, but my gut says I can trust him. I must trust him, with my leg, I have little choice... I need to go now sweet one. Remember always, that I've loved you since that moonlit night, Ben.*'"

Silence followed. Abbi swiped the blinding tears away. It wouldn't do Ben any good if she were to crash when they were so close to him.

"911? I'm calling to report that a police officer has been shot out on Moonlit road." Everyone looked at Noah but Abbi. A huge grin was pasted on his face.

"Mhm... yes just turn left at the crossroads, follow it to the white building. You can't miss it from the smell of skunks. My name?" Noah started fumbling with the speaker, "Sorry, you're breaking up..." he hit the end button.

Grinning, he looked up and saw all eyes on him.

Moonlit Road

"What?? It's the fastest way to get the cops to come."

"Good to know," Kim chuckled, as she wiped her eyes.

Abbi pulled the SUV onto the shoulder, angling it between the trees. She looked around before cutting the engine. It was the perfect spot. No one would be able to see it if they happened to look down the road. "Let's hope they get here quick." She nodded out the window.

Five hundred feet give or take a few, sat a low white building close to the road. The smell of skunks permeated the air.

"What should we do?" Ava whispered.

"I know what I'm not going to do." Abbi said, soundlessly opening her door. "I'm not waiting for the cops to show up." She quietly closed it and walked to the back of the SUV.

"Abbi get the hell back in the car." Noah hissed.

She ignored him. Opening the rear door, she looked in the compartment. *Where would I find the tire iron?*

Lifting the hatch of the cargo area, she found what she was looking for. Snatching it up, she tested the weight of it. Giving a self-satisfied nod, she looked up to see four sets of eyes staring back at her. "What?"

They all spoke at once.

"Mom. What are you planning on doing?"

"Abbi sweets, you can't possibly be thinking of doing what I think you're thinking of doing?"

"Abbi, I said get the hell back in the car and wait for the cops!"

Kim was the only logical one of the four. "Don't you dare leave without me!!" she said, scrambling out of the car. She joined Abbi at the back of the vehicle, poking around, she triumphantly whisper shouted, "Aha!" holding up the jack.

"What are you going to do with that? Change their tire?" Mark snorted.

Kim stood for a minute in thought. "Well... I'll whack them over the head." she said swinging it.

Mark rolled his eyes and looked at Noah. Both men nodded as they reached for their door handles, joining Abbi and Kim at the back of the SUV.

"If you're all going, I am too. But you can't just storm in there expecting to find Ben." Ava reasoned. "And why the need of weapons? How bad can it be in there?"

Abbi shook her head. "Ava, I'm not waiting another second, and they have guns. That's why I need you to stay here. Wait for the cops okay?"

"No, I'm coming. I'll be fine." Ava protested as she moved to slide out the door.

"Ava... I don't need you there," Abbi paused. That sounded horrible. "I meant... I don't need to worry about you too, okay? Please, just stay in the car, lock the doors and wait for the police." Not waiting for a response, Abbi closed the hatch with a soft thud.

"Noah, can you lead the way to that building?" Abbi jerked her head in the direction of it. "We need to get behind it, I think. Ben said there are cabins back there."

In a loud whisper he said, "Follow me, stay close. And if you hear gunshots for the love of God, duck."

Chapter 13

"**N**oah how much further is it?" Kim wheezed leaning up against a tree.

"Shhhh!" he said quietly to her, holding a hand out as he hunched over, peering through the trees.

"Do you see anything?" Abbi asked softly, squatting down, she too looked through the trees.

They were in the forest at the back of the building. The moon gave off enough light to see a row of cabins standing silent against the backdrop of more trees. Right in the middle of a clearing.

Abbi's breath caught in her throat at the sight before her eyes. There, a man and a woman were talking. Both had their arms raised, both with a gun in their hand. The man was pointing his gun at the woman's head. But the woman was pointing hers in the opposite direction.

So, who is she pointing it at?

Staring intently, Abbi silently moved closer to get a better angel. It was an old woman, it had to be Daisy! Dread filled her as she took one step closer. It felt like a cold icy hand, gripped Abbi's heart as her eyes fell on the man wearing a bright yellow coat. *Ben!*

Her heart dropped to the pit of her stomach. She had known with every fiber in her body who Daisy was pointing that gun at…but she didn't want to believe that it could only be Ben. Seeing him standing there with a gun aimed at him…

She had to act. She couldn't stand there a second longer and watch as the man she loved was shot through the heart. She scurried off towards the trio.

"Abbi get the hell back here!" Noah hissed.

"I'll get her," Mark called out in hot pursuit.

Abbi was within reach, just one more stride and Mark would have her. She stopped dead in her tracks, causing him all but to topple over her. Somehow, he managed to stop himself before hitting the ground.

"What the hell Ab...!" Mark was quickly cut off by Abbi's hand over his mouth. She pointed to the edge of the trees to her left as a second man exited into the clearing.

They watched in silence as he approached the gun happy group from behind. Mark turned to Abbi, a horrified look in his eyes. Eyes that popped out of his head when he saw the guy draw not one, but two guns from his waistband.

༄༅

Ben saw a figure approach from behind Dean and Daisy. *God please don't let it be Abbi...*

He breathed a sigh of relief when he saw Smitty come into view.

Smitty held a finger to his lips. Quietly he reached behind him with both hands. Quickly he brought them forward, a gun in each, one aimed at Dean, the other at Daisy. A twig snapped under his boot causing both to turn to face him.

"Why don't you gimme that gun there, before it goes off, hmm Daisy?" Smitty said, nodding at the gun in her hand. "Ben, get behind me," he called.

Without a word, Ben started to make his way over. With every step he took, he braced for the sound of gunshots ringing out; followed by a piercing pain. It felt an eternity, but he was almost there.

Daisy glared at Smitty. "What the hell is wrong with you?" Not moving an inch, she held fast to the gun, still aiming it at Ben. "This isn't part of our plan," her voice shook with anger.

"No, you're right, it isn't part of *your* plan. Now drop the gun!" he yelled.

"Why? What difference does it make if he dies now or at dawn?" she demanded as the gun shook uncontrollably in her hand.

Dean spoke up just then, "All in good time old woman. The Sheriff said dawn, he has his reasons for it I suspect."

"Shut up!!" She screamed. Motioning at Ben with the gun, "You know I have a job to do and it's to take him out by any means," she said as she took aim…

༄༅༄

Abbi and Mark were joined by the others at the edge of the clearing. All watched in stunned silence as both Daisy and the other man jerked around to the newest member of their gathering.

A soft sob escaped past Abbi's lips when she heard Ben's name. Holding her breath, listening to the gravel crunch under the slow rhythmic shuffling of his crutches was more that she could handle. Tears glistened down her cheeks as she watched him slowly come into view. The sight of him tore her to pieces, he looked broken in so many ways.

Abbi's eyes snapped to Daisy when she heard the woman screaming. As if in slow motion, she watched the old woman took aim at Ben.

Moonlit Road

"Nooooo!!" Abbi shrieked as she crashed through the trees, the others hot on her heels.

There was no way the gun happy group couldn't have heard them. The fierce cry of anguish that came from Abbi's very soul would have had the hounds of hell running in fear. They must have looked like crazed lunatics. Brandishing their weapons as they came into the clearing to the sound of sirens approaching in the distance.

The welcoming sound of the police didn't stop Abbi, she went straight for Daisy; the only one that had held a gun to Ben's head. Her only thought was to cause as much pain Ben had endured at their hands, to her. The fact that Daisy swung the gun in her direction didn't stop her either. Abbi wanted to maim her, pull her hair out from the roots and then punch her in the face. She might even throw the tire iron at her.

Ben stood rooted to the spot.

Abbi don't you see the gun in Daisy's hand? Seeing that look on her face, he knew he had to stop her.

"Abbi, no!" he yelled, launching himself in her direction just as a shot rang out. He didn't make it in time. He watched as Abbi collapsed on the ground. Her blood pooling onto the ground.

Memories of them together flashed through his mind like an old family video on a projection screen. An animalistic howl of pain came from Ben as he fell to his knees by her side.

His tears mingled with Abbi's blood on her beautiful face. He checked her pulse... nothing. He gathered her into his arms, rocking her back and forth while his screams of agony echoed in the clearing.

The anguish he felt a moment before only intensified the malice he was now feeling. He set his venomous stare on Daisy. Tenderly laying Abbi on the ground, he slowly rose to his full height... without the aid of his crutches. He heard a loud gasp behind him. Thinking it was Kim reacting over finding Abbi, he forged on.

Mark knew what Ben was going to do. He had broken up a fair share of fights in his lifetime. Ben's included. Despite what the circumstances were, he knew Ben could never live with himself if he took out his anger on a woman. Especially a little old lady.

Mark grabbed him from behind, wrapping an arm around his chest he pulled him back. "It's not worth it buddy, you can't do this. She's an old lady." Mark said hotly against the back of Ben's neck.

Ben fought to loosen Marks grip. Truth be told he didn't have the strength to do so.

"She isn't an old woman! She's wearing a mask." Ben spat, still twisting and turning trying desperately to get out of Marks grasp.

Kim came around them, with tears in her eyes she said, "No Ben. You can't…but I can." She put her hand on his chest, shoving him back.

Kim promptly turned and sneered at Daisy, "You're lucky she's alive. You better hope she stays that way, bitch!" she ground out, flinging the jack she was still holding at Daisy like it was a shot put.

Daisy cried out in surprise, not expecting a solid steel object being flung at her, she dropped her gun and tried unsuccessfully to catch it before it crashed into her. She failed miserably, howling in pain as is landed on her foot with a sickening, bone cracking thud.

Ben grabbed Kim by the arms just as the first of many police cruiser pulled into the clearing.

"Kim, did you say Abbi's alive?" Ben asked, his eyes red rimmed.

Kim nodded. "She must have had the wind knocked out of her when she hit the ground. Didn't you hear her gasping?"

Mark gave a tug on Ben's arm. "Hey, how come you remember her, but you don't me?" he asked.

Moonlit Road

Ben shook his head in answer to Kim and ignored Mark as he stumbled to Abbi's side. He laid his head against her chest. Holding his breath, he prayed Kim was right.

A single tear slipped across the bridge of his nose, blinding him momentarily. He closed his eyes as he felt Abbi's heartbeat, steady against his cheek. A shuttering sob escaped past his lips, when he felt her hand make its way to his hair, stroking it softly.

"Abbi. Abbi, can you hear me?" he looked up at her face. His hand made its way to gently cradle her head as if she were a newborn baby.

"Ben?" she mumbled, opening her eyes. She tried to sit up. Wincing as the pain shot through her head. She put a hand to her temple, feeling a sticky warmth. Confused, she pulled her hand away and looked at it. Blood. "What happened?" she asked.

"You were shot. A bullet grazed your head," he said, gently gathering her in his arms. He inhaled her scent deeply as he held her. "You weren't breathing... just bleeding. The medics are here now." Ben whispered as he put an arm under her knees and drew her to his chest.

"I've got you sweet one." He stood up, holding her as the paramedics came with a stretcher. Gently he laid her on it and backed away. Watching as they worked on her.

Mark came to him. Putting an arm around Ben's shoulder he gave it a squeeze.

"She'll be all right buddy. What about you though? Shouldn't you be getting looked at yourself?"

Someone shouting prevented Ben from answering him.

"Let me through! I need to see my mother now!" Ava shouted, shoving at the police officer blocking her way.

"It's okay Billy, let her through." Smitty yelled to the police officer.

"Ava, over here," Mark waved her over towards him and Ben.

"Ben!" She flung herself at him, hugging him with all her might. "I'm so happy to see you're safe."

"It's good to see you Ava," he said. Taking a step back, he set her at arms length, his eyes full of worry were focused on something over her shoulder. "Ah I need to know. How was your mom, while I was gone?"

Ava turned her head and glanced to see what Ben was looking at. The medics were wrapping a large white bandage around Abbi's head.

Not that he doubted for a minute that she missed him. His only concern was it hadn't affected Abbi too drastically. It didn't matter to him one way or the other. Nothing could kill the love he had for her. He needed to know if her feelings were the same for him.

"Honestly?" Ava raised a questioning brow at him. He looked at her and nodded.

"Well. I've never seen her so upset in my life. She was going nuts. I saved mental health crisis numbers in my phone just in case. You have no idea how many times I almost called them."

"What stopped you?" Ben asked.

"We never left her alone." She sighed and pointed towards Abbi, "I'm just going to go over to her now." She excused herself and left.

"Ben, can I ask a question?" Mark looked directly at him.

Ben looked at him and nodded, "Of course."

Ava returned before Mark could get a word out, she put a hand on Ben's arm she said, "She's asking for you."

Torn between going to Abbi's side and Mark he said, "Please tell her I'm coming. I'll just be a moment." Ben turned back to Mark, "You were saying…?"

"How come you know Ava and Kim, but you don't have a clue who I am…" he asked frowning.

Moonlit Road

Ben stood in thought. Finally, he said, "You know, Abbi and I never did go on that date you paid for." The relief on his friend's face was all Ben needed to see. He gave Mark a smirk as he limped towards the ambulance.

Stopping he turned and looked at Mark. *I wonder...*

"Ah... Mark? Does the name Everett mean anything to you?"

Mark looked taken aback. "Doesn't it to you? Ben, buddy. That's your stage name..."

Ben frowned, "Oh, right. Um, aren't you coming?" He asked, jerking a thumb towards Abbi.

"Wouldn't miss it for the world."

He put an arm around Mark's shoulder as his friend joined him. "Say... do you still have that box I gave you on the plane?"

"Box?" Mark raised his brows in question. "What bo... Oh shit! I gave it to Abbi. She has it!"

"Right... Well, I'll just go buy her a new one then."

As they passed a police cruiser, Daisy was screaming from the back about her rights for medical attention.

"Ma'am, right now you will need to wait your turn. You gave up your rights when you killed an FBI agent. And attempted to kill two innocent people." The police officer slammed the door shut and walked to Dean and Smitty. Muttering to them about the loud one in her car. Ben's step faltered. *Wait a minute... Why is Dean not in a cruiser...?* His question was answered when he saw the flash of a metal star on Dean's belt.

His thoughts were interrupted from a quick jab of Mark's elbow to his ribs. They had arrived at the back of the ambulance.

"Hey," Ben said softly, his eyes matching his tone. He looked at her laying on the stretcher, the blue blanket tucked to her chin. She was beautiful to him even with her bandaged head and pale skin.

"Hi." A smile tugged at the corners of her lips.

"Sir?" A small female voice spoke behind him. He turned and looked down. "My name is Allison I'm a medic. You're injured, too aren't you?"

Ben nodded. His leg was hurting, but nothing close to what it had been. It must have only been sprained. The bulge under the skin had been nothing more than swelling. With absolutely nothing to do, the past week and a half gave it time to heal he supposed.

"We will take you along with Abbi here if you're okay with that. Hop in." Allison waited until Ben climbed in and sat down. Slamming the door shut, she went around to get in next to her partner.

"Do you know who that is Reece?" Allison asked as she shut her door and buckled up.

"Yeah. That's Ben Everett. Awesome actor," He said, clearly star struck.

Allison wrinkled her nose. "Who? What…no, I meant the lady." She said smiling. She too was in awe of who they were transporting to the hospital in Gatlinburg.

"Oh…no, I have no idea," he said as he steered down the winding dirt road.

"It's Abbi Stevens… The author of the Jasper Killings?" She smiled as she turned to check on their patients. Her heart melted at the sight of them. There, Ben sat on the floor, his head on Abbi's chest, staring at her while he spoke softly. Their hands clasped as he stroked her hair with his other.

Allison turned back in her seat. "Someday, I hope to find a love like that." she sighed wistfully as the ambulance made its way down the moonlit road.

Part Two

Chapter 14

Ben couldn't take his eyes off her. She mesmerized him. If he had any doubts before of where he wanted his life to take him, it was all clear as crystal now. Wherever Abbi was, he was home.

Trying desperately to stay awake, Abbi rubbed his back.

"Ben?"

"Yes, love?"

"Hold me?"

"Of course, sweet one." he whispered as he rose off the floor. Feeling weak as a kitten, she moved towards the wall of the ambulance with his help. Ben laid down beside her and gently wrapped her in his arms. She laid her head against his chest wincing at the pain it caused, but nothing was stopping her from being held in his arms.

"After we leave the hospital, can we please go home?" She asked, her eyes fluttering shut.

She was so incredibly tired. Bone tired. She felt Ben shift. Opening one eye she looked up at him, mere inches from her face.

"Yes love. The bullet just grazed you from what the medics told me. So as soon as you're released to travel, we'll go home." He kissed the tip of her nose, "Sleep now, I'm not going anywhere anymore." he murmured as he pressed his lips to her hair.

She didn't want to sleep. She was afraid that if she did, it would all be a dream, like so many before.

She looked up at him again. The tears she had held on to for so long now threatened to spill over at any second.

"I've missed you so much. I thought that you were gone forever," she sniffled.

"I've missed you too. Now, hush love. I'm here." He kissed her tears away. "I promise, I'll never go anywhere without you again." His lips trailed to her ear, along her jawline to her mouth.

Abbi welcomed his touch. She instantly melted against him as he deepened the kiss. A bump in the road, reminded them exactly where they were.

He leaned back and stared at her.

"I can't stop looking at you. You're the most beautiful person I've ever had the privilege of knowing. On the inside and more stunning on the out.

He laid a finger against her lips when she was working on arguing the fact. "Shh, I never say anything I don't mean. And I meant every word of it." he gazed into her eyes. It was time.

"Abbi…I wanted to do this the proper way. Me on one knee, with a box in my hand." He paused. "But I'm not waiting another second for things to be perfect."

Abbi reached under the blanket, blindly searching for her jacket pocket. Fumbling, with the blanket, she finally got her arm free. She opened her hand, revealing a small box within.

"Is this the box? Mark gave me this when he was still in the hospital. He made me promise not to open it and to give it back to you when we found you." She looked up at him through her lashes. "I swear I didn't open it."

He grinned. "I believe you love." Ben took the box from her hand. With her still wrapped in his arms, he opened it.

Moonlit Road

There siting in the middle of the velvety box was a band of silver. A stunning diamond sat nestled in the middle, encircled by peridots and topaz.

"Oh…!" Abbi softly said in awe. She quickly looked at him.

Ben took a deep steadying breath and tried to settle the racing of his heart. *Why am I so nervous?* Deep down he knew why. They had never talked about marriage before and he was afraid of her answer.

He swallowed hard. "Abbi, will you give me the greatest honour of my life in becoming my wife?" He held his breath, waiting for her answer.

With him looking so lovingly into her eyes, Abbi wondered how she could have ever doubted his feelings for her. *Wait… Did I hear him right? He did not just ask me to marry him…did he?* Abbi was speechless as tears ran from her eyes.

She shook her head slowly from side to side, her eyes never leaving his. When she saw the disappointment flash across his handsome face, her face crumpled. She quickly explained, "Dear lord, I didn't mean no! You shocked me; I didn't know it was an engagement ring. Mark never told me," she babbled.

She took hold of his coat, giving it a slight tug, she urged him closer. Smiling, she whispered, "Yes. I will," and tenderly laid her lips on his.

Her kiss stole his breath away as he inhaled her intoxicating scent.

The ambulance pulled to a stop. "We're here guys." Reece called out as he put the gearshift in park.

"I better get a move on it hadn't I?" Ben moved off the stretcher and kneeled beside it, taking the ring from the box. "Shall I?" he asked, taking her hand in his.

She nodded, a soft smile on her lips.

Gently he placed the ring on her finger. "I had it specially made," he said softly, looking into her eyes. "The diamond is for

April, the month we met, and the first time I fell in love with you. The topaz is for November, your birthstone. And the peridots are for…"

"Your eyes." Abbi breathed. "They remind me of your eyes."

He chuckled, "No, it's my birthstone."

"I know, but they still remind me of your eyes." She smiled as the back door opened.

"Let's get you folks looked at, shall we?" Reese said, reaching to unlock the wheels on the stretcher. He said to Ben as he pulled Abbi from the back of the ambulance, "Mr. Everett, you sit tight. Allison will be right back with a wheelchair for you."

Everett…Everett

Ben thought a wheelchair was a little extreme but nodded, "Sure thing." It gave him time to be alone with his thoughts.

Something had been bugging him since the farm. What was it that Daisy had said? She'd had a job to do… *Clearly it was to kill me but who ordered it and who was she talking to on the phone that night?*

He dared not mention it to Abbi. Then again, she may have heard it the way she had come charging at Daisy like she had. That was another thing… Who the hell was Daisy? He felt a hand gently shaking his arm. Glancing down he saw Allison there, an empty wheelchair waiting beside her.

Concern was etched across her face. "Mr. Everett? Are you okay?"

"Ah. Yeah. Sorry." he sighed, heaving himself off the seat.

Allison hurriedly grabbed his arm. "Here, let me help you."

Together, they managed to get him settled in the chair. Allison unlocked the wheels, just as a blinding light flashed in their eyes.

"Dammit! Who the hell told them?" She muttered, turning Ben around so that her back was all they could see.

"Is that a photographer?" Ben queried, looking around Allison to see.

"No, it's the paparazzi. They have been hanging around the hospital since the crash, waiting like vultures."

Quickly she wheeled him into the emergency department, down a hall and stopped at the nurses' station. Nodding towards the doors that her and Ben had just come through, she said. "You might want to lock those doors and get security out there. The scavengers are back…" All at once four nurses jumped up, running for the doors.

Allison nodded, pushed the wheelchair forward and said, "Now. Let's get you to Abbi."

※

She was sleeping when Ben was brought into her cubicle. A doctor was standing over her looking at her chart while a nurse checked her vitals.

"Hi Doc. This is Dr. Anderson," Allison whispered loudly to Ben. "This here is Ben, he's with Abbi." She pushed his wheelchair next to the bed. "He needs his leg looked at. Looks to be either a bad strain or possibly a hairline fracture. He was walking on it." She looked around at Ben "Right? You were walking on it?"

He nodded. "Yes. A bit." he said.

"Nurse, can you order an x-ray for Mr.…. ah…" Dr. Anderson flipped through the papers Allison had handed him. He looked at Ben, questioningly.

"Quinn. Ben Quinn," Ben supplied.

"Mr. Quinn, please?" he finished addressing the nurse.

Dr. Anderson came around the foot of Abbi's bed to Ben and knelt in front of him.

"Any pain or swelling?" Not waiting for a response, he pulled up Ben's pant leg and felt along his calf muscle. Frowning, he looked up at Ben, "How long has it been like this?"

"Ah. It happened in the crash. About a week and a half now?" Ben answered.

"I don't think it's too serious, you were able to walk on it. The x-ray will tell us more." He stood up and wrote on a chart. "We ordered some blood tests on Abbi; they should be ready by the time you come back from the imaging department."

"Will she be okay?" Ben asked anxiously, looking at her still form.

"The bullet grazed slightly above her temple. She's lucky, any lower and she wouldn't be here." The doctor said solemnly.

"There was so much blood..." Ben said, staring blankly at the memory.

Dr. Anderson nodded in agreement. "Head wounds will do that. My concern is when she fell. Did she hit her head or land on her stomach?"

Oh god, is he worried about internal bleeding?

"Um." Ben thought for a second. "Neither. She just kind of crumpled. Like she passed out. She did land on her back, but I don't think she hit her head."

"She wasn't breathing, is that right?"

"Kim. Her sister said the wind was knocked out of her. I thought she was gone..." he blinked the sting away as he relived the scene in his mind.

Ben watched, as the doctor wrote on Abbi's chart. He was doing an awful lot of writing.

When he could no longer stand it, he asked, "Is there a problem Doctor?"

Dr Anderson, put her chart on the peg at the end of her bed. He turned and looked at Ben. "No, not at all. Just want to make sure her levels are where they should be and that they keep rising. She will be moved to a private room. I'll keep her for a couple of days to monitor her blood periodically throughout it."

Ben frowned. "Levels? What sort of levels?"

The doctor smiled "Why, her hCG levels of course.".

"And they are…?" Ben hedged for an answer.

"To make sure she doesn't miscarry." The doctor stated.

At this point Ben was totally confused, shaking his head he squinted. "Miscarry? What does she miss carrying?"

Doctor Anderson let out a bark of laughter. "You know… a baby?" His brows rose on the last word.

"Oh." Ben nodded his head. "Okay…Wait…" He half stood up. "A *what?!*"

Glancing at Abbi, laying so peacefully there. A smile widened on his mouth. He couldn't believe what the doctor said. "Y.. You mean she's pregnant? You're saying that I'm going to be a father? You said that, right?"

"Well. I guess you are if you and she are together. Yes, that's what I'm saying." The doctor nodded. Walking over to the door he stopped and said. "Now that we have that covered. Congratulations! Nurse Murray, will give you a tetanus shot and take you to x-ray."

Ben looked at the nurse who was standing there with a syringe in hand and beamed. "I'm going to be a father."

"So, I heard. Congrats. Now stand up there and drop your pants."

Ben did as he was told. The stupid grin never faltered from his face; not even when the needle jabbed into his butt cheek.

Chapter 15

Dean had just left. He had stopped by wanting to see how Abbi was doing and left his card. And told Ben to reach out if either of them needed anything.

Ben was still reeling from the shock of finding out the man was a DEA agent. He was still trying to wrap it around his head that Dean's tough guy act had been just that, an act. Ben told him he should get into acting; He was that convincing.

Now he was sitting beside Abbi's hospital bed, watching the steady rise and fall of her chest. The day nurse Paige had brought him in a reclining chair after he refused to leave her side. Paige said it was of the utmost importance to keep his leg raised. The x-ray revealed a fracture of the fibula. The wrap job that Daisy did had at least saved it from further damage. Luckily, he was on the mend, and the walking boot cast would allow him to walk without the need of crutches most of the time.

As he watched her sleep, he couldn't help but think of his timing to ask her to marry him; before either of them found out about the baby. Otherwise she might have thought that was the only reason he'd asked.

Maybe she already knew? No. She would have told him he was sure of it. Her groaning in her sleep had him on high alert.

Ben quietly put the footrest down on the chair. Moving to the edge of the seat, he waited to see if she would stir some more. That way he could be there for her if she did. He watched as a frown appeared on her face, while her legs kicked at some unforeseeable force.

He gently leaned on the edge of the bed and reached for her hand. Leisurely he traced circles on her palm, as his other hand reached to smooth her hair back from her face. A single tear ran from her closed eyes. His thumb followed the path it made, making him want nothing more than to crawl into bed beside her and hold her. He'd already tried that and was told he couldn't. The real reason for the chair being brought in for him, he suspected.

༺༻

Abbi so desperately wanted to reach out to Ben. That bitch was between the two of them. Holding a gun to his head; preventing her from reaching him. She had to do something, anything to stop her from shooting him. She watched in horror as the bullet sliced through the air in slow motion, only stopping as it plunged into Ben's chest…

She screamed his name and bolted upright in the bed.

Ben jumped back causing the bed to shake. "*Bloody hell, Abbi!*" he nearly shouted, remembering the last second that they were in a hospital. Softening his tone, he murmured, "Love, are you okay?" One minute he was drying her tears, the next she was screaming at him.

She was scaring the hell out of him. She was looking through him, not at him. "Abbi? Honey are you okay. Do you want me to get the doctor?" He stood for a moment, nodding, he said, "I'll get the doctor."

"No! I'm fine, it was just a dream… a nightmare," She said finally coming to her senses.

He wasn't convinced she could see him. The way she had looked at him, as if he wasn't even there.

"Really Ben, I'm fine. Can you get me a drink of water please?"

Moonlit Road

"Sure, love." he went to the table on the other side of her bed to fetch her a glass of water.

"You're walking! What did they say about your leg?" She asked as he held the glass to her lips.

He chuckled, "I am yes. It's on the mend. Got myself this fancy boot." He showed his leg to her as she took a sip.

She felt terrible. Here she was lying in a bed while he limped around with a cast on his leg, waiting on her. But goodness she was exhausted. She tossed the covers aside. Intent on getting dressed and going home.

"Um Abbi, where are you going?"

"Why home. I'm going home Ben. Where are my clothes?" she asked, slowly coming to a stand.

"In the closet, but…. ah, you can't." he said moving to stand in front of her.

"Of course, I can. I'm fine. A bit woozy but I'll come around." She said, moving around him, headed to the closet.

"No, you need to get back in bed. You know, you lost a lot of blood." he said, gently turning her around back towards the bed.

"Ben don't be so silly. It's time we went home."

He didn't want to come right out and say Abbi your pregnant, but what little choice was she giving him? The doctor had to monitor her levels.

A moment of panic seized him. *What if she doesn't want a baby?* He never thought about that. She already had kids, grown ones; would she want to take care of a newborn after so much time had passed? He suddenly felt sick to his stomach.

As much as he loved the idea of being a father, he couldn't make her have his child… or could he? No! He wasn't the one that would be pregnant for nine months. Despite that he loved the idea of being a father; he loved her more. If there was any risk to her, he would refuse to allow her to take it. He was being selfish in that respect. But so be it. It was settled at least from his point of view. He would only support her decision if there was absolutely no risk to her.

"Love, you need to sit down. We have to talk." He said softly.

Abbi looked at him, really looked at him. He was scaring the hell out of her. Was there something so terribly wrong with her that she didn't know about?

"Ben... what's wrong? Am I sick?"

Maybe he's sick?! Oh no... No! She couldn't handle it if he were. Had everything taken a toll on him more than she'd realized? Now she felt such an incredible guilt. She sat down on the edge of the bed. Staring down at the ring he had given her. The ring he so thought-fully had made just for them. She breathed in a shaky breath and searched his face, "Are you?"

"God no!" he hurried to reassure her. He sat down on the bed beside her, pulling her close he said, "No Abbi, neither one of us is." He smoothed his cheek on her silky hair careful to avoid the bandage. He took her chin in his hand turning her face upwards, to look into her eyes.

"Then tell me why I need to stay." She felt like she was on the verge of tears, like a tired child being told no. She pleaded, "Why can't we go home right…"

His mouth covered hers swallowing the rest of her words. Someone coughed loudly. Ben broke off the kiss, leaning his forehead against hers, he sighed. "One second," he murmured, brushing his lips where his head rested seconds before. Abbi watched as he went to the door, talking in a hushed tone to the nurse standing there, a plastic caddy in her hands.

Ben closed the door soundlessly and returned to sit back down beside Abbi.

"What the hell is going on Ben?"

"Um." He scratched his head, wondering just how he was going to tell her. He pointed to the door. "She'll be back."

Abbi raised her brows. "Okay… *And?!*" She watched the play of emotions cross his face as he stared at the opposite wall. What really confused her was the stupid grin on his face. She watched as he physically wiped the smile off his face with his hand, finally, he turned to her.

"And… ah." he stopped. Feeling confident, he steepled his fingers… quickly he leaned forward rubbing the bridge of his nose.

Nope I can't bring myself to say it. What if she's mad? What if she blames me, then what? He shook his head. No, she wouldn't do that.

"Ben for the love of God, will you just *spit it out*?" She raised her voice he noted on the last three words.

His eyes snapped to hers. She was getting a bit upset he could see. He took a deep breath, took her hands in his and rubbed his thumbs back and forth, hoping her anger would diminish.

He looked deeply into her eyes and said "Abbi… we never talked about this. Ever. But." She looked so beautiful staring at him. *Why am I worrying when she looks at me this way?* A smile tugged at the corner of his lips. "We are going to have a baby, you and I."

Oh no… he watched as her face went from serene to scrunched up confusion, then shock. Her body began shaking uncontrollably. He watched as she leaned forward clutching her stomach. *The BABY!!*

Afraid she would topple onto the floor he grabbed her from behind. That's when he realized she wasn't in shock. On no not Abbi. No. Her shaking turned into a low cackling that turned into a full belly laugh. Her clutching her stomach, was in mirth.

She gasped, "Oh Ben!" She looked at him then. Her eyes glistened with tears from laughter. "You're pulling my leg aren't you!" she giggled.

He bit his lip, a small smile started at the corners of his mouth as he shook his head no. Her face fell. She saw the moment when he saw the horrified look she felt on her face, mirrored in his eyes.

Slowly shaking her head, a small gasp of denial escaped past her mouth as he nodded.

Licking his lips, he said softly, "Come here love." He gathered her into his arms, rocking her gently, as her body wracked with silent sobs.

Good lord... The man I love tells me I'm pregnant, with his child and I laugh in his face. He must... hate me.

Abbi felt crushed as she pulled away from Ben's comforting embrace.

A baby?! But how? She couldn't be... could she?

She felt like an idiot. The woman was supposed to tell the man.

Her mind raced going over the telltale signs. *How did I not know?* With her past pregnancies she had always known.

Good Lord. I'm 45 soon to be 46. I'm too old to have a baby!!

She needed to escape, to think, to work this out in her mind. She needed to be alone. She needed... to go home.

She got up from the bed and stalked back over to the closet. Yanking the door open, she tossed her belongings over her shoulder onto the bed.

"Abbi! You can't leave." Ben said quietly watching her.

"Watch me." She said stripping off her hospital gown.

Standing naked before the window, she heard Ben exclaim, "*Good God woman!*" As he hurried over to the window, snapping the curtains shut.

"Love, they need to monitor your titter levels." He stood there, hands on his hips, head tilted to the side, staring at her belly. "Only for a couple of days." he tried reasoning, softly.

She snickered, yanking her shirt on over her head. "It's titer levels Ben. And they can do that in Canada."

Moonlit Road

He reached out a hand to rub her back, stopping himself, instead he quietly said, "Abbi... please."

His tone had her freezing. With one foot in her pant leg, she turned around to face him, her eyes shooting to his.

The look on his face tore at her heart. She dropped her pants in defeat as she sat heavily on the side of the bed. She couldn't do this to him. This was his child too. And truth be told, she was being selfish. As silly as it was; she didn't want to share him with anyone. Aside from all of that she was scared. Scared as hell and wanting to dart out the door back to the safety of her home.

Ben sat beside her. He dared not touch her, knowing how she could at a moment's notice go off and run from him. Never to stop running. The thought terrified him.

"Love. You are the single most important thing in my life. Never doubt that for a minute." He took hold of her shoulders. "I know you're scared; I am too..." He took her hand then. Tracing circles in her palm, he continued. "I'm afraid of losing you. I'm also afraid of you walking out that door and never looking back."

Is he nuts?! Yes, I want to run out the door, but never to return to him? No. I will always return to him.

"Ben... I..." He took her face in his hands, guiding his mouth to hers. As one hand slipped to cradle her head, she felt his desperation in that kiss. His fear, his worry and his love for her. He pulled away, searching her eyes with his fevered ones.

"Abbi, what I'm trying to say is that for me, your health is paramount. I don't want you having my baby if it means I could lose you. That almost happened last night. I'll never take that chance again." Just him uttering those words was almost his undoing. His eyes teared up. "You're okay with that right?"

She nodded sadly. Reaching up, she wrapped her arms around his neck. She laid her head against his strong chest as their tears flowed freely.

She needn't have worried. Ben knew her all too well. Or maybe it was his love for her. Deep down she knew what was scaring her, and it wasn't her fear of sharing him. She was carrying a life... their child's life. Ben knew she wouldn't be able to make that decision herself if it came to that. He knew that she could never do it. He was her rock, her light and voice in the storm once again.

A small cough announced someone at the door. "Excuse me...I really need to be taking your blood now."

"Abbi?" Ben whispered.

She nodded, pulling out of his embrace. She slowly got up. The nurse must think she was nuts. Wearing nothing but her shirt as she pulled the blankets back. She silently crawled back into bed and pulled the covers up to her chin.

As the nurse came to her side, she bit her lip when she saw the needle. The hand that slipped into hers, lightly traced back and forth. Ben. His ever-soothing touch was always there when she needed it most. She glanced at him giving him a watery smile.

No wonder she had been so emotional lately. Her hormones were through the roof. She gazed at him as she felt the needles sting. Watched the emotions play across his face, the instant empathy he felt for her. If she had ever had any doubts before, in that moment she knew he would be a loving husband to her and wonderful father to their baby.

She made up her mind. No matter what, she would have this baby for him.

Her biggest fear was also her biggest secret, one that he knew nothing about. She had to tell him. She just hoped that they found out who was trying to kill him first...

Chapter 16

Abbi raced down the aisle, making a beeline for the washroom. She was having a terrible time going home. Foregoing the long drive, they had decided the quickest way to get back was to fly straight to Toronto. And good Lord, she had to do it sober.

She slammed the door and knelt before the commode. The first wave of nausea turned into her upchucking the contents of her breakfast; courtesy of the Gatlinburg hospital. The thought of throwing up in a public toilet, especially one so confined as the airplane's had her retching for a solid ten minutes. She leaned back against the door, praying that was the end of it.

When she felt it was safe to move, she grabbed hold of the sink. Shaking like a leaf, she had to claw her way to a stand up. She was so incredibly tired, and she needed a drink. Preferably a gin and tonic but the tonic would have to suffice. She splashed water on her face, hoping that would wake her up a bit.

Sighing she took a hard look at her reflection in the mirror. She frowned.

My God I look old.

Her eyes grew large as she saw a man materialize behind her in the mirror's reflection. *Well, you have been to hell and back, Abbi. What did you expect?*

Spinning around, she saw that she was alone. Not only was she tired she was now hallucinating and hearing voices.

She snatched a handful of paper towels in disgust and patted her face dry. She froze as her ring sparkled in the mirror. A sudden fear gripped her chest tightly and it had nothing to do with the plane. Something was wrong, terribly wrong.

✣

Kim leaned around Mark to look at Ben. "Where is Abbi? We are close to landing; she needs to get back here." she told him.

"She ran off to the washroom." Mark answered. He looked across Abbi's empty seat at Ben, "What's taking her so long?"

"I'll go see," Kim said.

"No. It's fine, I'll go get her." Ben got up and slowly maneuvered down the narrow aisle with his cast. He wasn't up to answering any questions from the others. Abbi and he had decided to keep her pregnancy quiet for now... just in case.

"Abbi?" he knocked on the door. "Love, we are close to landing."

Abbi took a steadying breath. She felt so clammy and dammit she was dizzy. Swiping a hand over her face she winced as her hand brushed the wound on her temple. A reminder of what she feared most, the possibility of losing Ben. She cleared her throat, "I... ah. I'm coming." She unlocked the door and pushed it open to see Ben standing there.

He lifted a hand and tucked a stray curl behind her ear. "You okay?" he murmured.

Not wanting him to see the fear in her eyes she nodded and quickly ducked under his arm and headed back to her seat. He watched her make her hasty retreat. Now wasn't the time to question her about anything.

Ben made his way to his seat and noticed the grip she had on her armrests as he sat down. He reached to take her hand, to offer her comfort but thought better of it. He smoothed his hand down his pant leg instead.

Neither of them said a word as the plane slowly descended towards the ground. Ben sat looking straight ahead, not wanting to look at her for fear she would bite his head off. Relief washed over him as he felt her small hand reach for his. Turning his palm up, he clasped hers in a reassuring grip. As the landing gear engaged and the plane taxied down the runway, he risked a glance at her.

She sat there, green to the gills and as beautiful as ever. He brought her hand to his lips, kissing it softly. She slowly turned, a soft smile on her lips. Which he immediately saw turn into horror.

Ripping her hand free of his, Abbi frantically searched for the vomit bag. No matter how many times she swallowed the bile refused to back down. There wasn't time to make it to the washroom; passengers were already preparing to disembark. And no vomit bag was in sight. She ripped open her purse, sticking her face inside of it she promptly threw up.

"Oooh. Myyy. GOD!" Mark yelled, horrified at what he'd just witnessed. His eyes grew larger by the second as he desperately scrambled backwards, up and over his seat. "What is *wrong* with you Abbi?" He hissed, standing on the seat behind his.

"For cripes sake Abbi. You just threw up in your purse!" Kim stated the obvious.

"Mom are you okay?" Ava asked concern written all over her face.

"Of course, she isn't *okay*, Ava." Mark spit out, tossing a hand towards Abbi. "She just puked in her purse! Who does that?!" He said, disgusted.

"Enough!" Ben cast a warning glare at the lot of them. "Come on love… lets go home." He murmured as he took her hand. She followed him down the aisle as the rest of them sat there staring in shock.

Moonlit Road

I will never fly again... Abbi thought mortified; tears stung her eyes as she followed Ben off the plane. She didn't care if he wanted to go to England, she would take a ship and meet him there in a month.

"Whoa..." Noah was the first to break the silence. "Is Ben always like that?"

"No, not usually." Kim said thoughtfully with a raised brow. Something was going on with Abbi and Ben. She knew it, just the vibe she was getting from them. And she was determined to find out.

෴

Once inside the airport terminal Ben headed straight for the car rental agency.

"Abbi, didn't you say that you drove part way?" He looked at her. "Where is your vehicle?"

She leaned on the counter for support and propped her head in her hand. "I called Lane from Tennessee and asked him to pick it up from the hotel for me." Abbi watched as he signed two rental agreements.

"Why two?" She nodded to the papers on the counter.

He kissed her on the tip of her nose. "Because we are travelling the rest of the way home...alone. But before we head there, I thought we'd stay a night or two here in Toronto. If you're okay with that?"

As much as she wanted to get back to her own bed, the idea of being alone with just him sounded perfect. Once they were home, there would always be someone around.

She smiled and nodded her agreement.

"Come on. Let's break the news to the others." He said grinning as he held the door open for her.

"Ah... there they are." Ben said pointing to Mark and Kim. The two were looking in opposite directions.

Kim turned just as they were approaching them.

"Where the hell did you guys go?" She asked. "We've been looking for ages for you two."

Abbi glanced around. "Where is Ava and Noah?"

"Washroom." Kim stated. She was uncomfortable. She wanted to say something but was weighing the reaction her words would have... from Ben.

"Look guys," Mark started. "I'm sorry for my actions back there on the plane." He shrugged and pursed his lips "I've just never seen anyone..."

Abbi stuck her hands in her back pockets and rocked on the balls of her feet. "Throw up in their purse before?" she said raising a brow.

"Yeah... that." He blanched.

"It was either that or your lap." Abbi smirked.

Mark uncontrollably gagged at the visual.

Ben let out a bark of laughter. "She's got you there, mate."

"I'm sorry too." Kim muttered just as Ava and Noah returned.

"Hey guys," Ava hurriedly said. "Noah was just saying he heard on the news that..." she turned to Noah. "What was her name again?"

"Gwendolyn Pearce." Noah supplied.

Ava nodded. "That's right! Anyway, she escaped police custody."

Mark frowned. There weren't too many people he knew with the name Gwendolyn, but he knew at least one. He was about to speak when Ben and Abbi said in unison "Who?"

Noah stepped forward; he held his hand out to Ben. "I'm Noah Steel by the way. We weren't properly introduced with all the hoopla that was happening." Ben took his hand in a firm grip, he still wasn't sure who the guy was, only that he knew Abbi from the past.

Abbi looked between Ava and Noah. "Does someone mind telling us who this Gwendolyn is?" she asked.

Noah sighed as he looked down into her eyes. "She's the one who shot you Abbi. She's Daisy…"

Abbi stood in stony silence. *Is that why I felt something was wrong on the plane?*

"What do you mean she escaped? How?" Ben asked, scowling.

"Well, after you two left for the hospital. The place was stormed by every agency possible. The US Marshals, ATF, DEA and FBI. The place was shut down by the way, with the sheriff being towed off to jail as well. Anyway. She was locked into the back of a cruiser or so everyone thought. When the officer went back to his car…she was gone. The only indication that she had been there was a silicone mask, her coat and…"

"She couldn't have gotten far?" Kim interrupted. "Not in that cold at least…"

"Normally no. What everyone is thinking is that she slipped under the radar. With the disguise that she was wearing, it was simple to do." Noah explained.

Abbi stood there in a daze. *What was the 'and' part Noah didn't finish?* She wasn't the only one to catch that, as she noticed a dark look pass over Ben's face. "And what?" he asked.

"Uh… and a message, written in lipstick on the window…"

Abbi clenched her teeth. "Spit it out Noah. What did the message say?"

"It's not important Abbs."

Noah saw the warning, flash in her eyes. He swallowed hard, taking a step back.

"It said 'I never leave a job unfinished.' But don't worry, I'm sure she'll be caught soon... hopefully."

Ben took Abbi by the arm. "Come on love, let's get out of here." They started walking away when he stopped. Turning around he tossed a set of keys at Mark. "Here, we'll meet you at home in a few days."

"What?!" Kim hurried around them to block their retreat. "Where are you two going?"

"To a hotel. Just for a few days." Ben sighed. Kim of all people should understand that. "We need this time...alone, Kim." He raised his brows to her.

Nodding, she said, "Sure, I get it." Now how would she figure out what was going on between them if she couldn't analyze their every move? She threw her arms around sister. Looking at Ben over Abbi's shoulder she said to him, "Promise me you'll take care of her."

Ben nodded. "You have my word."

Taking a deep breath, Kim ran her hands down Abbi's arms to take her hands in her own and gave them a squeeze. *What the hell is that?!*

Her eyes shot to Abbi's left hand. Kim's eyes bugged out of their sockets as she stared at the ring on her sisters' finger. She looked at Ben, a smile on his mouth.

"You didn't even tell us!" Kim cried. She looked at Abbi. "You didn't tell me!" she squeaked, accusingly.

"With the hospital and all, I never even thought Kim. I'm sorry." Abbi said tiredly. She was starting to feel the bile burn in throat again.

Abbi glanced at Ben, locking eyes, she sent him a silent message.

"Right." He nodded. "We have to be going now Kim. And now you know why we need to be alone." he chuckled, waggling his eyebrows at her.

She blushed three shades of red. "Of course. You two go and enjoy yourselves. We'll see you in a few days."

As they walked away Abbi promptly stopped and fumbled with her purse.

Kim could be heard excitedly telling the others in a sing/song voice, "We're gonna have a wedding."

If Abbi ever stops throwing up, we will... he thought. "Love, let me help you." Ben held her purse while she once again stuck her face in it. "All good?" He asked, passing her a water bottle.

She shakily nodded, taking a sip. "Yeah." She wiped her mouth on her sleeve. "Thank goodness my wallet is in my pocket. I think I need a new purse. No amount of laundry soap is going to get that clean."

Ben chuckled. "Don't ever change my love. Come on. Let's go buy you a new purse."

Chapter 17

Abbi flopped onto the hotels bed, sinking deep into its opulence. Ben had gotten them the best suite available. When she protested telling him all she needed was a bed and him, he countered that they would be there a few days and wanted to make the most of it.

A soft satisfied purr came from her throat as she snuggled into the mattress beneath her. She needed a cat nap was all. Just a tiny one she thought as her eyes drifted shut. She felt the bed sink beside her as Ben laid down next to her. She was too tired to even look at him. She was exhausted from everything.

After the doctor had given her the go ahead to travel it had been a hurried frenzy of activity. Racing to get to the airport, her anxiety had her on high alert for the flight back home. The dreaded trip to the washroom brought a bad taste to her mouth just thinking about it.

"Love, do you want the fireplace on?" Ben murmured.

Abbi melted at his words. Damn. There it was. That sexy way he had of saying things. *Oh, how I've missed it…*

Abbi bolted upright, wide awake looking straight at the fireplace.

"Oh my God, I knew I saw that man somewhere!"

Ben scrambled to sit beside her. Brushing her hair away from her eyes he asked, "Are you okay? Please don't throw up on the bed!"

She sat in a daze.

"Abbi?" Ben took her by the arms and turned her towards him. "What is it?"

She snapped her eyes to his. "Ben. I need to tell you something. You're going to think I'm crazy…" She nodded rapidly, "And that's because I likely am."

He laid back against the pillows, motioning for her to come to him. Pulling her close he said, "I won't. I promise. Now, tell me, what is it that has you bothered so?"

"Before we went to you…" She shoved a hand in her hair. "I can't believe I forgot to tell you any of this."

"It's fine. You've been through a lot the last few days." He murmured, resting his chin on her head.

"Right." She nodded. Taking a deep breath, she began. "We had gone to the crash site. I had to see it for myself…" She looked at him and laid a hand on his chest. "Despite already talking to you and knowing you were gone, I had to make sure you weren't there."

"I'd have done the same thing."

"Good."

He chuckled at her response. Urging her to continue he waited for her to begin.

"After Mark and I came back from… where you had landed, the local police where there. A lot of them, at least five cars. We thought maybe they were there to arrest us. But it was because Noah had called them." She shook her head. "Anyway, I was asked to go sit in a police car with an officer. Nice lady… she offered me cookies. I think it was a bribe so I would sign her copy of my book." Abbi frowned, "Which reminds me," titling her head she stared at the opposite wall. "… it's still in my purse."

Ben raised his brows, a smile breaking on his lips. "You mean…" He looked at the purse, a giggle bubbled up from his throat.

She slowly nodded "... Yeah. That one. I'll need to send her a new copy."

"I'll say!" Ben knew that wasn't the end to her story, "Go on, love."

"I realized something was wrong when I saw the look on Mark's face." She looked at him then. "I tore out of the cop car and demanded to know what was going on... Do you know what that creep Sheriff Martin said to me?"

Ben saw red at the mention of the Sheriff's name. He stiffened as his eyes took on a menacing glare. Quickly, he buried his nose in her hair masking the look from Abbi's eyes. He thought back to the last words the two had exchanged. What he wouldn't do to be in his prime physical condition, standing in front of the sheriff now and he say what he had about Abbi then. He would beat the bloody hell out of him.

She backed away and searched his eyes. Laying her hand along his jaw she said, "What's wrong Ben?"

He licked his lips, "Nothing, sweet one. Go on."

He was lying she knew it. Not lying exactly, more so protecting her from something.

"Okay. Well, he said it was an open investigation and he wasn't at the liberty to discuss it. Anyway. I need to get to the point of my story; this stuff is all so trivial now."

Ben chuckled, looking at her he saw the tiredness etched on her face. She was so lovely. He leaned close to her, taking her chin in his hand, he brought his mouth mere inches from hers and whispered, "I agree," before lightly brushing his lips against hers.

Abbi saw stars. This man could melt her in seconds. It was crazy how her body reacted to his touch. "... Yes. Um. Well, I tore out of there threatening to leave everyone behind. We raced down the highway. I had no clue where I was going... South was where I was headed, as if drawn to go to go that way. We ended up in a small town called Martinsville. At some creepy looking B&B. The owner opened the door as if she were expecting us."

Pausing she scrunched up her forehead. "Come to think of it… she did know. She was expecting us. She called me by name."

"Really?" Ben looked at her curiously.

"Yes. Her name is Hester Riley."

Goosebumps ran up Abbi's spine when she said her name.

Ben leaned over, towards the foot of the bed and grabbed the comforter pulling it over them as he laid back against the pillows.

She sighed in delight at his thoughtfulness.

"So… is that it?" he asked when she said no more.

"Yeah no," she shook her head. "There's more. This is the crazy part…"

Ben looked at her, waiting for her to continue. She smiled at him, taking hold of his hand.

She was stalling he could tell. "Abbi just tell me. I promise I won't think you're nuts." He grinned.

"Fine!" She cleared her throat.

"Abbi," He said in a sexy, warning growl.

"Okay!! After being there a few days, I'd just sent you a text…waiting for your response. Mark was chatting away. He wanted to know what I had stuffed in my pocket. It was my book." She looked at him. He wasn't following her she could see, needing to explain she said, "The cops' book. Anyway, he went off to bed because I was ignoring him, while I was reading the book. There was something bothering me… about it."

"Oh?" Ben squinted at her; his brow furrowed. She reached up a hand to smooth the lines. It wasn't working…

She waved her hand away when he kept looking at her. A question in his eyes. "That's a whole other story that I'm too tired to tell right now."

"Okay," he chuckled. Truth be told he was getting tired too… But he had to wonder if that was why everything seemed so familiar about the time at the farm… Her book.

Moonlit Road

"So anyway, Hester scared the crap out of me. She had been sitting there the whole time apparently while I was reading." A nervous giggle slipped past her lips.

Ben caught it, knowing exactly what it meant. She was getting scared. He gripped her hand tightly, tracing circles across the back. He sat there silently waiting for her to muster up the courage to go on.

Abbi sucked in a steadying breath. Still not believing what had happened at that old creepy house.

"Hester… She asked me if she could tell me a story. I said sure," Abbi laid her head on his shoulder and snuffled closer. "She told me about the man she fell in love with. And then she told me how to find you. Gave me precise directions. The name of the road. Even what the farm looked like… the smell of it."

She coughed; a tickle started in her throat. Leaning over him she grabbed a bottle of water from the nightstand. Taking a long swallow, she capped it and tossed it on the bed.

"How?"

"Franklin. Her love. He told her to tell me."

Ben's brows shot up. He'd heard Abbi crying out that name the last night at the farm. It's what woke him. He shrugged his shoulders. "Why couldn't he just tell you himself?"

"Mhm. One would think he could, right? Wrong…He was killed in the war… he came back to her." Abbi said, curling up beside him.

He leaned back to look at her. Softly he said, "He came back to her? As in how, Abbi?"

She didn't answer, instead she placed her chin on his shoulder, and said, "I didn't believe a word of it, of course. Until…He knew about your note. This one…" She reached into her bra where she kept it close to her heart and handed it to him.

Ben unfolded the paper. He knew what was on that note. He had written it countless of times. Whenever he flew, he'd write it over again, tucking it into his seat. He read it anyway… One moonlit night…

He held it up. "Did anyone else know about this?"

Not that I'm having doubts about her story, but maybe one of the others had mentioned it?

"Mark was there. He found it but didn't read it until after he handed it to me."

"Right. It's not likely something Mark would talk about anyhow. Especially to a stranger, an odd one at that, by the sounds of it." he sighed.

"That isn't what convinced me," Abbi said. "I mean I thought the same as you; someone mentioning it. But, no."

Ben looked at her, searching her eyes he asked, "Then what did?"

"Franklin said I had to hurry…you didn't have much time."

A tear slipped from the corner of Abbi's eye. Ben laid a hand along her neck, his thumb rested lightly in front of her ear. Holding the side of her face, he watched it as it trailed down her soft cheek. He leaned forward, catching it with his tongue. He ran his thumb along her jaw, stopping to rest it just below her bottom lip. Gently he lifted her chin, bringing his face within inches of hers.

He was going to kiss her. Abbi knew it, she yearned for it…welcomed it. But first she had to finish telling him. "He knew what I wanted for Christmas, Ben." He pulled back, still holding her in his arms. Shock registered on his handsome face.

He searched Abbi's face for a reaction, looking deeply into her eyes he asked, "You told no one?"

She shook her head no. "I swear, I didn't breathe a word of it to anyone. Only you." She said softly.

He laid back against the pillows, pulling her with him.

Abbi laid her head on his chest, listening to the steady beat of his heart. She could feel his hand drawing circles across her back. He was lost in his own thoughts, she knew that.

He either thinks I need to be locked up or he's coming up with a logical explanation…

"Love. You didn't answer me before. Tell me. You said Franklin came back to her… He came back to her as in how?"

"As in a ghost, Ben." She tilted her head up to look at him. "He also came to me in the washroom on the plane. I thought I had recognized him. When you mentioned the fireplace, it came to me…Hester had pictures of them together on her mantel." She laid her head back down. "You don't believe me, do you?"

It was a ghost. It was Franklin that had visited me. Waking me…but why?

"Yes, I do Abbi. Tell me. Was he clean cut in one of the photos? About 24 years old?"

She snapped her head up. "Yes… How do you know?"

He caught a stray curl. Twirling the silkiness between his fingers, he said, "Because the night you came, and I had decided to leave. I woke to you crying the name Franklin in my ear… he was in the corner of my room. He told me, not out loud but in my mind, that it was time to go. He was wearing his uniform, Abbi…"

A misty chill overcame the room just then. Instantly they were both off the bed bounding into the living area of the suite.

"Shall we go out for a bite?" Ben smacked his hands together.

Nodding rapidly, Abbi was already heading for the door to get her shoes on. She snagged up her new purse along the way; and the bag it came in. *Just in case…*

Chapter 18

"How bout dinner and a movie in instead?" Ben chuckled, catching her by the hand before she could dart out the door.

"Come here love." He said silkily, twirling her towards him, she landed hard against the length of him. Her eyes growing large as his arousal pressed against her.

He searched her face for pain. She had collided with him hard.

"Are you okay?"

"Lord, yes!" she said breathlessly.

He smiled and murmured, "I love you Abbi; no ghost is stopping us," he growled, dipping his head to capture her mouth. He kissed her the way he had so desperately been dreaming about since being reunited.

She dropped her new purse on the floor, moaning as she wrapped her arms around his neck. She opened her mouth in response to his seeking tongue.

Ben grabbed the back of her thighs and hiked her up as she wrapped her legs around his waist. Never breaking contact with her sweet mouth, he carried her to the sofa. Laying her gently on it, he covered her face in soft kisses. Running his tongue along her jaw to her ear. She sighed in pure delight when his teeth lightly grazed the sensitive skin there.

It had been so long since he held her in his arms like this. Abbi couldn't get enough of him, his touch, his mouth, his scent all made her dizzy with wanting. She leaned her head back, arching her neck to his seeking lips that caused her insides to liquefy.

She had to feel him, skin to skin. Tugging on his shirt she pulled it up over his body as she lightly trailed her nails along the hard ripples of his stomach. She felt exhilarated when his muscles reacted to her touch.

Grinding his arousal against her, he just about passed out from the pain it caused in his leg. It was in the way. He couldn't stay in this position any longer, half on the sofa half off.

Panting, Ben groaned out, "Abbi…"

His voice drunk with passion, caused her nerve endings to hum all the way to her core. Cold air met her as his heat moved away. She opened her eyes. Something was wrong.

"Ben! What is it? Is it Franklin?"

"What? No. God no. It's my leg," he grimaced, in pain. "I'm sorry love. It's locking up on me." He felt like a piece of shit, doing that to her. She had been ready to fly out the door and he'd stopped her. Now their night was ruined in more ways than one.

"Don't be silly. You have nothing to be sorry for Hun." She kissed him then. Taking his breath away with just her lips.

"Let me get your crutches." She jumped off the sofa in search of them. "You should be using them all the time you know," She chastised him, as she walked back to his side. "Here. Let's get you into the shower." She sent him a sly smile, "My new puke bag will cover your leg perfectly. I'll order some food. Chinese sound good to you?" She asked looking at him.

"Sounds perfect." He nodded.

"Good I'll do that while you get undressed." She guided him towards the bathroom. A padded bench sat alongside the wall near the tub.

"Um…there's no shower in here." Ben stated the obvious.

"A bath it is." Abbi said. Whipping out her cellphone she called room service. She walked over to the massive tub and turned it on as she gave their order. Sitting her phone on the vanity, she turned to Ben.

"You're still dressed!" She said grabbing his pant leg.

"I am, I was too busy watching the ravishing vision before me," he grinned at her.

"Were you now?" she chuckled.

"Mhm. You know love," he waited for her to look at him. Nodding he said, "That tub is big enough for the both of us." He sent her a sexy grin. "And I could use a hand. You know, to hold my leg up…or something."

She managed to get his pants off. She decided not to take the boot off, she didn't want to hurt him anymore than he already was.

Abbi put a hand on each of his knees, pushing his legs apart she stood between them. Leaning down, she lightly she traced his lips with the tip of her tongue.

"One step ahead of you handsome." She smiled against his mouth, as she shimmied out of her pants.

Reaching for the hem of her shirt she pulled it off in one fluid motion, followed by her bra. She gasped as his tongue flicked out, lapping at her nipples. His hands went around, squeezing her butt, drawing her towards him as he sucked one then the other.

Good lord, she wasn't expecting the sensations his mouth caused within her body. She knew what he did to her, but this was different, more heightened, more exhilarating.

She held tight to his head. Knowing any second, she was going to go off like a rocket. She had to take control right now and get him in the tub. She moaned as his fingers slipped under the leg of her panties and inside her. That was it, that's all it took. Leaning her forehead against his, she clenched every muscle in her body in response to his touch, shaking uncontrollably, she had an asinine thought at that very moment, *I've never had an orgasm while standing before.*

Dropping her forehead to his shoulder, she opened her eyes, looking directly at his erection. Problem was, he still had his underwear on.

She slowly brought her head up, looking into his eyes, she could see the fevered passion in them. Gripping his boxers by the waist she whispered, "Lift up."

He did so silently, knowing exactly what she was thinking.

Pulling them off him, she slid her panties to the floor.

Abbi straddled his legs, holding onto his shoulders she slowly settled herself in his lap. Eye to eye they looked at each other. Concern flooded his eyes.

Would it hurt her this way, or the baby?

Knowing it would go deep, he had to ask her. "Are you sure love?"

Biting her lip, she nodded as she raised up on her knees, slowly lowering herself onto his shaft. Ben couldn't contain the hiss that emitted past his lips as her wet warmth enveloped him. Somehow, she wrapped her legs around him, drawing him in as deep as she could. He wanted nothing more than to grab her by the hips and ram into her softness, but he held back. She had to be in control...

Ben took hold the back of her neck and brought her to him. His lips sought out the spot behind her ear. He knew it drove her crazy when he touched her there. Flicking his tongue along her ear, his voice thick with passion he groaned, "For the love of god Abbi, if it hurts you, stop. Because I can't."

In response she held him tight as his mouth devoured hers, she slowly rode him, quickening the pace when his hands cradled her back. Trusting him, she leaned against his strength while his mouth suckled at one breast than the other. Holding his head to her, she could feel him coming ever closer to his release.

Increasing the pace, she clenched him with every stroke until as on, they both shuddered in spent pleasure.

They held each other afterwards, both lost in their own thoughts.

Ben was blown away, as usual. Every time they made love, she always amazed him.

Why the hell do I leave her for months on end… just to film a movie?

He knew he said it before and yes maybe he was having second thoughts about quitting acting. But this, this that just happened between them? Hell no, he wasn't leaving her again. He never wanted to miss a second of his life with her.

"You okay?" He murmured, looking down at her.

"Yeah. Sorry," she mumbled. "I'm getting up," She took a deep breath and untangled herself from him. Not wanting to leave his arms, she turned quickly to the tub, wiping her eyes, hoping Ben wouldn't see her tears.

Abbi bent down, shutting the taps off. The water was close to overflowing. Lifting the lever, she waited to gain her composure as the level slowly lowered. She heard Ben hobble over to her side. Felt his lips softly touch her shoulder.

"What's wrong love?"

The tone of his voice had her tearing up again.

How can he read me so easily?

Was she really that transparent? She liked to think she wasn't.

Abbi took a shaky breath. She might as well tell him. It was time she revealed her secret.

Methodically, she lowered the lever, plugging the tub. Turning, she looked him in the eyes. The strength she felt in his gaze gave her the courage to tell him.

The look of fear in Abbi's eyes had him scared. She ran her hands through her hair, and said, "Ben. I'm terrified…"

"Of what?"

"Of everything."

He raised a hand to touch her. "Abbi, you have no reason to be."

Shrugging off his hand, she darted behind him and stalked to the door. Grabbing a hotel robe from the hook, she slipped her arms in and tied the sash tightly at her waist.

"I do. I'm sick with worry knowing that crazy bitch is on the loose. I'm scared that whoever put her up to this will never be found…" she stopped.

Ben watched as she stood there, not more than five feet from him. He studied her face. *I couldn't be more in love with her if I tried...* She looked at him then. Her soft gray eyes changed like storm clouds gathering on the horizon as she violently started to shake.

"What is it?!" Ben pleaded.

Abbi bit her bottom lip, trying desperately to stop its quivering. She didn't want to say it. "I…I don't know if I can have our baby Ben…" She covered her face as her tears ran down her cheeks, the memories from days gone by flashed through her mind.

"What? Why?" he went to her. "Love, you can tell me. Just say it."

"I…when I told you before about my ex. It was all true. We had been slowly drifting apart for years. There was no longer any love between us when we ended it. I was in love with him, when the kids were small, I won' t deny it… but. He killed that when I lost the baby."

Baby? Ben stood up straight, inhaling sharply. His eyes glistened. "I see." He couldn't help being affected by what she just said. He felt like such an ass. His heart went out to her and yet he couldn't help but feel jealousy because she had loved another.

"No, you don't! I was far into my pregnancy. He blamed me! Said it was my fault! My fault that his child had died, like it wasn't mine too." she sobbed. "Do you have any idea what it's like to carry a child? A child that you know will never take a breath on its own, to full term?!" She started to pace. It wasn't Ben's fault her ex was a first-class asshole. "Of course, you don't." She shook her head sadly. Quietly she continued, "I had to deliver my baby… alone. With no one there to lean on, no shoulder to cry on. He wasn't even there for the funeral. He just swept it all under the rug as if it never happened."

Ben didn't say a word as he pulled her into his arms, stroking her back as her sobs wracked his soul.

How could any man act so… Heinous to the woman he loved?

"Abbi, I promise you, I'm not your ex." he soothed.

She leaned back, looking at him with her tear stained face, her eyes puffy from crying.

"Ben, I know you're not. But," She swallowed hard. "If the same thing happens this time, and who knows with my age. I couldn't bear it. I'm more terrified of losing you, of you blaming me, than I am of any risk to my health."

"Love. It will never happen. I promise you." He lifted her chin with his hand. "I will be there every step of the way. If history repeats itself, I'll never leave your side. As a matter of fact, I promise you'll have to beat me off with a stick," he smiled softly. "And even then, I would never leave you," he murmured. As light as a feather, he brushed his lips against hers.

Leaning back, she looked at him in awe. *What did I ever do to deserve this beautiful man?*

Softly she returned his kiss as her tears flowed freely. *Good lord will I ever stop crying around him?*

Honestly, she didn't care, she would cry the rest of her life if it meant she could always have him. Someone up there must have known she needed him in her life. Whoever it was she silently thanked them.

Chapter 19

They were on their way home after a blissful three day stay in Toronto. Ben had wined and dined her, they went shopping, and sightseeing and both were ready to go home.

He had insisted he could drive. His right leg was perfectly fine he'd told Abbi. They had an hour worth of driving left to get to Pearl Lake and he was starting to feel the effects of being cramped up. He hated to admit it, but he couldn't finish the drive. He had to switch with Abbi. Taking his eyes off the road for a second, he glanced her way. She was leaning back in her seat. Her arm bent at the elbow, rested on the door with her head propped in her hand. Staring at him.

"What?" He laughed looking back at the road. Licking his lips, he said, "Tell me something. How long have you been watching me?"

"For the last twenty minute or so."

"Oh yeah...?" he nodded. He cocked an eyebrow and sent her a suggestive smile. "Do you see anything you like?" A sexy smile flitted on his mouth as he took her free hand, bringing it to brush it against his lips.

"Always." she responded in a throaty purr. "So...When are you going to pull over so I can drive?"

"You can tell, can't you?" He looked at her. She just nodded. "Right. The next town we'll switch."

"Fine, but if you need to stop sooner, we can pull in someone's driveway." she suggested, looking out her window.

It had snowed since she'd been away. When she'd left home in search of Ben, the fall colours were out in full force. She shook her head. She couldn't believe she'd been away for almost a month.

Her birthday was in less than two weeks, a month before Christmas. She wanted nothing for either days. *I have everything I want right here in the car* she thought sleepily as her eyes grew heavy. She fought the urge to rest them as the scenery sped by.

Abbi awoke with a jerk from the vibration of her phone coming from her pocket. Fumbling with it, she answered with a tired, "Hello?"

"Mom?! It's Ava. Where are you guys?"

Abbi noticed the panic in her voice. Bile rose in her throat as she was instantly taken back to the day Ava raced into her house to tell her of the plane crash.

She hit the Bluetooth button on the cars' display to connect her phone to the speakers. She thought it silly of Ben to link it to a rental but now was thankful he did.

"Ava, what's wrong? Honey slow down."

"You need to get home right now. Someone shot Brutus with an arrow."

Ben stepped on the gas. There was no time to stop now.

Abbi felt her world spin out of control. Not Brutus, her dumb sweet hero.

"What happened, Ava?" Ben asked.

"I don't know. We let the dogs out about an hour ago. Molly and Lucy came back." Her sniffling came through the speakers, "They wouldn't come in. They kept barking and running away.

Mark said they looked like they wanted us to follow, so we did. We're at Mack's right now, him and Doc are working on him."

"We'll be there in about a half hour. Stay put at Mack's. We will meet you there." Ben told her.

"Mom? I'm so sorry." Ava cried into the phone.

Ben glanced at Abbi. She was sitting there clutching the phone in her hand, staring straight ahead, as tears streamed down her face.

"Ava, your mom can't talk right now." He reached over and took the phone from Abbi. "We'll be there in twenty minutes." He disconnected the call and frowned in thought.

Ever since I came into Abbi's life it seems I've brought her nothing but pain.

"Love?" He looked at her again. The look she turned on him sent a ripple of dread over him.

Is she thinking the same thing?

"We'll be there soon. You okay?"

"Yeah." She nodded.

"What is it? "He was afraid to ask but he had to. "Please. What are you thinking?"

She looked at him blankly. "What am I thinking?" Her mind raced. All that kept running through it was this was all too familiar. Too familiar because she wrote it.

Someone was after them; and they were getting it all from the Jasper Killings…

Abbi whipped her head to look at Ben. She put a hand on his arm.

"Tell me. You should know. Does this not all feel eerily familiar to you?" She raised her brows expectantly at him.

He gave a slight nod. "Yeah, a bit. Why? What are you thinking?" He asked, driving up the hill that would bring them into the village of Pearl Lake.

Frustrated, Abbi groaned.

It was there, she knew it! But for the life of her she couldn't put her finger on it. When she was back at Hester's house reading the bit about the train crash, she felt it then too. She shook her head. She must be having brain fog from the pregnancy. She needed to read her book from beginning to end. But first she had to get to Brutus.

Ben pulled the car to a stop outside of Mack's store. Abbi scurried out in a flurry. Glancing back, she saw Ben struggling to get out of the car.

Racing back to his side she opened the back door and took his crutches, holding them impatiently while he maneuvered out the door.

"Thanks. Sorry for that. Go!" He mumbled his apology; he knew she ached to get to her dog.

She instantly felt like a bitch. Wiping the frown from her face she gave him a watery tired smile.

"You have nothing to be sorry for Ben. Come on." Despite wanting to race to the back door, she kept his pace, holding onto his waist so he didn't slip on the snow and ice, until the last five feet, when she let go and hurried inside.

It took a second for her eyes to adjust from the blinding snow. When they did, she saw Brutus was lying on his side; a white bandage was wrapped around his middle. When he saw her, he whined, raised his head and cried at the sight of her.

"Oh, my poor baby," she rushed to him. "Stay Brutus. Lay down baby." She crooned softly to him as she hugged him tight.

"Hey Ben." Doc nodded.

"Hi. How is he doing?" Ben came to the side of the table and laid his head on Brutus. The dog thumped his tail and turned to give him a sloppy kiss.

Moonlit Road

"He'll survive. The arrow missed everything vital. He might have a bit of nerve pain in the future. Time will tell." Doc told them as Mack came into the back room.

"Ben, Abbi! So good to see you two again." Mack boomed. "I hear there is a big surprise soon. Congratulations!" Mack smiled.

They both looked up at Mack at the exact same time. Confusion and shock on their faces.

"Surprise?" Ben raised his brows at Abbi. A 'who did you tell about the baby?' look crossed his face.

She shook her head, silently conveying she didn't.

"Yeah," Confused over their reactions, Mack motioned to the front of the store. "Ava said you two were getting married."

Relief was evident on both their faces.

"Right, right! Yes. Abbi said yes." Ben nodded, grinning.

How did we both forget that?

Abbi looked up in surprise. "Ava is here?"

"Yeah, she's manning the store while we tended to Brutus here." Mack told her.

"Ben, could you?"

He could tell she was fighting a battle; wanting to stay by Brutus' side and going to see Ava.

"Of course, love. Go. I'll stay with him."

Abbi bent to give her dog a kiss on the head then left in search of her daughter.

Ben turned his attention on Doc and Mack. He knew something was up but didn't want Abbi to know… at least not yet.

"Now that she's out of the room," Ben cast his eyes between the two men. "Will one of you tell me what the hell happened to him?"

Mack gave a heavy sigh. "It was no accident Ben. Someone deliberately shot him."

Squinting, Ben said "How are you so certain that it was done on purpose.

Doc opened a drawer. "Here." He passed the feather end of a broken arrow to Ben.

"Turn it over Ben." Doc said gravely.

Ben scanned the surface as he turned the aluminum arrow with his fingers. He frowned. There was writing scratched on its surface. He traced the words with his thumb… 'Hollywood… you're next'. Ben tapped it against his hand, testing the weight of it. "Who else knows about this, what's written on it?" he asked.

Both men shook their heads. "Just us Ben, and whoever wrote it," Mack answered.

Ben nodded, a scowl on his face. "Let's keep it that way please. Abbi doesn't need to know."

He had a feeling he knew who was behind it. He just needed to prove it.

Chapter 20

"Did you send the warning like I told you?" The caller asked.

"Of course, I did... I told you I had it in me." She blanched at the memory. The dogs yelp, searing through her mind, would stay with her a long time.

"Excellent! Now, lay low."

"Wait! Are you going to tell me now who you are and who is behind all of this?" she asked.

"I'll contact you in a few days with further instructions." an audible click was heard.

She looked at the phone in her hand. "What a bastard." She muttered to herself. "Lay low?! In this God forsaken town?" The man was pure evil...

ಬಿಂಚ

Ben watched from the door as Mark carried Brutus into the bedroom.

"Here, Mark. Lay him down here." Abbi said, tossing a pillow aside, allowing him to lay Brutus on the bed. She crawled up beside the dog and put her head on his chest.

"You two go, we'll be okay now, won't we buddy?" She crooned, smoothing her hand down the dogs back.

Moonlit Road

"Sure, thing love. We will be in the kitchen if you need anything, just yell." Ben said, covering her with a blanket before following Mark out the room.

Once in the kitchen Mark went to the fridge and grabbed two beers. "I stocked your fridge for you," He said, popping the caps on both, he passed one to Ben.

Ben took it, looked down at the bottle in his hand and said, "This wasn't a random act Mark. It wasn't a hunter who accidentally shot Brutus. This was on purpose. Whether they were aiming for him or one of the other two, I'm not sure, but it was a warning." he pulled the arrow from his back pocket and laid it down on the counter.

Mark looked down at it frowning. "This is it?" he raised inquisitive eyes to Ben. Seeing him nod, Mark picked it up and examined it.

He read the message carved in the arrow. "Do you remember that actress I dated a year ago?" Mark asked, studying the feathers.

A snort came from Ben's direction. "Which one?" he grinned.

"The brunette." Mark said quietly.

There had been a few brunettes if Ben's memory served him. "Briefly," he shrugged. "Wait, was it her you were with at that restaurant in France?" Ben squinted.

"Yeah, that's the one. The only time you met her." Mark paused. Looking up from the arrow, he looked Ben in the eye. "I really thought she was the one. I thought I wanted to marry her. I was a fool."

Ben leaned against the counter and crossed his arms. "Why? I thought you two had hit it off rather good."

"Yeah... so did I. That was until she saw you that night. After that, she had made you her mission."

Ben looked at him in disbelief. "That's insane Mark. I've never met the woman outside of that day." Ben saw the look on

Mark's face. "Man. I'm sorry, I had no clue. Not that it would have mattered if I had known." Ben trailed off.

Mark waved a hand. "I know you didn't." He laughed, "Believe me. It was for the best. Luckily, I dodged the bullet with that one. If I had known she was capable of something so... so repulsive... I... Thank God I broke it off."

Ben raised a brow, "Where are you going with this Mark?"

Mark held up the arrow. "This. I'm going with this. That girl I dated was a champion archer, she was known as The Piercer. She could pick the dimple off a gourd fifty feet away..."

"A... Gourd? What the hell does a gourd have to do with all this? And what does *she* have to do with it?"

Mark sighed, took a swallow of his beer and looked at his friend. "Her real name was Gwendolyn Heed. She changed it to Pearce... for acting purposes."

Ben rubbed his jaw. Dawning flashed in his eyes as he pieced the puzzle of Marks words together. "The Piercer... She's Gwendolyn Pearce. Otherwise known as... Sonofabitch! She's Daisy..."

"That night at the farm I wasn't paying attention to her. Even in her disguise I likely could have picked her out in a lineup. Is there any way you can get a hold of the agents who were there?" Mark asked.

"You mean Smitty and Dean. I suppose I could try."

"You could try the local department back in Tennessee, but they didn't seem to know too much of anything." Mark said.

Ben hobbled over to the coat rack. "I think I stuffed one of their cards in a pocket." he said rummaging inside. The doorbell suddenly chimed above his head, he stopped and looked up at it.

"Are you going to just stare at it or open the door?" Mark asked.

"Right." Ben said pulling his hand from his coat pocket. Looking down he saw he held Deans card in his hand. Pulling the door open he was shocked to see the man standing in the flesh.

"Well it's about damn time," came that unmistakable drawl of Dean.

He stood there leaning, a half grin on his face as Smitty walked up behind him.

"How…?! I was just going to call you," Ben stated. Stepping back, he held the door open for both to enter.

"Were you now? I guess we beat you to it." Dean said, folding his sunglasses, stuffing them into his pocket as he took in his surroundings.

Mark reached into the fridge and produced two more beers. He handed each of them one. "What are you two doing here?" He asked.

"Thanks, my man. Cheers." Dean tipped back the bottle taking a long swallow.

"We have reason to believe that Gwendolyn Pearce is headed this way. She was spotted at the border." Smitty said looking at Ben. "Ah… Unfortunately, we didn't have a photo of her without a disguise to alert them before she slipped through."

Ben frowned. "How long ago was this?"

"Day before yesterday." Dean answered.

A hushed silence fell over the room as Abbi could be heard calling Ben from the bedroom.

"Excuse me." He muttered, as he headed to the hallway. He stopped, turning around he said, "Don't any of you tell her what's going on."

"Ben, she has a right to know…" Mark said as the two cops nodded their agreement.

"Not a word. I'll tell her myself." *When the time is ready*, he thought, turning down the hallway.

Mark looked at both men. "Sorry about him. He's been a bit off since... well everything. So, are you two staying in Pearl Lake or something?"

"Yeah, if we can find lodgings. Is there a motel around here?" Smitty asked.

"Nope, everything closes up for the winter. Well there is the cabins, but they aren't heated. You likely would freeze come morning. This place is big enough, but I can't speak for Ben and Abbi." Mark nodded towards the window. "You could always stay over at my place on the sofas."

"Might just take you up on the offer." Dean said. "We need to stay close by in case she decides to show up. Staying in the car out front isn't an option."

Mark held up a finger. "Ah, about that." He marched over to the counter where the arrow laid. "This was in Abbi's dog. I think it was Gwendolyn who shot him."

Dean looked at him, taking the arrow in his hand, "You don't say?"

"What makes you think that Mark?" Smitty asked, whipping out a small notepad and pen.

"I dated her last year. She's a marksman in archery. Plus, she had the hots for Ben."

Dean raised his brows. "If she was interested in him, then why go after him?"

"Wait... She never acted like she even knew him, and he had no clue who she was. She took her disguise off in front of him. I was there." Smitty said pointing to his chest.

"That's just it, she's an actress, a convincing one at that. The whole time we dated she told me she wanted him. They met once, very briefly in a restaurant we were dining in," Mark sighed. "And... you guys didn't know this, but Ben had amnesia while there. Whatever it is, she's a first-class bitch."

"Amnesia huh?" Smitty looked thoughtful. "So, is it fair to say that she really isn't after Ben… but Abbi?"

Mark sighed. "I think she's after both… Why else would she shoot the dog and write that?" He pointed to the warning on the arrow.

Frowning Smitty, took the arrow and nodded, "Good point…"

Taking a swig from his bottle, Dean nodded, "Ah… we'll take you up on your offer Mark."

ಬಂಞ

"Hey, my sweet."

Abbi smiled as Ben laid down behind Brutus. He gazed at her over the dog's head as he stretched out a hand to catch one of her silky curls.

"How is he?" He whispered.

Brutus thumped his tail against Ben's leg. The dog looked up at him, giving him a sloppy kiss.

"Better," Abbi grinned. "I thought I heard voices?"

"Yeah, you did." He twirled the strand between his fingers, marveling at the softness. "Dean and Smitty are here. They're in the kitchen talking to Mark."

Ben saw the concern flash across her face. "Oh? Did they say why they came?"

Of course, she would ask… *What the hell do I tell her?*

"Ah… Well. Maybe. You called for me before that was discussed" God, he hated lying to her. But did he really have a choice?

"Okay." She pushed herself up to a sitting position. "I guess I should get up."

Moonlit Road

Ben put out a hand. "Are you sure love? I mean…" he trailed off when she gave him a look.

Giggling, Abbi said, "Yeah… I'm sure. Besides. Brutus needs to go out, I think. He's been letting off some godawful farts."

Ben laughed. "Yup, I'll say that he needs to then." He moved to the edge of the bed. Putting his arms under Brutus, he slowly raised him off the bed.

"Good Lord put him down. I'll call for Mark." Abbi said, scurrying around to help if the need arose.

"It's fine love. I can get him. The leg is already feeling better." He lied of course. But he needed her to come with him, having her hear about Gwendolyn wouldn't do. "Just open the doors for me, will you?"

She jumped off the bed and crossed the room to the French doors. Pushing them wide, she followed Ben to the yard as he gently placed Brutus on the ground, panting from the exertion.

Abbi searched his face. "Are you okay?"

"Yeah I'm fine." he looked towards the lake. "Just need to catch my…. Sonofabitch!!"

Brutus let out a low warning growl.

"What?!" Abbi cried in confusion, following his line of view, horror filled her face.

"Get in the house Abbi. *Now!*"

She didn't listen, she ran towards it. It wasn't the fact that the dock was on fire. No. It was the fact that a publicity poster of the Jasper Killings was in the middle of the inferno on a wooden sign and written across it, were three words… 'YOU'RE NEXT ABBI'.

Chapter 21

It was December 1st. It had been less than two weeks since the dock fire and one week since Abbi's birthday. Everyone had come with birthday wishes. Kim had baked a cake and Luke and Lane had called promising to be there for Christmas.

She said no presents and threatened to throw them in the lake if someone went against her wishes. It didn't matter that the lake was frozen, she'd cut a hole in the ice and shove them in if she had to. Ben had wanted to take her to the city, but she had insisted the time they had spent in Toronto was her birthday present.

Brutus was well on the mend. His strength was returning steadily, no longer needing to be carried to do his business in the yard. Ben's cast was off. His leg still hurt from time to time but had healed nicely and Abbi was over her morning sickness. The only thing hanging over their heads was the fact that Smitty and Dean were staying between their house and Mark's. There was no sign of Gwendolyn, not since the fire. Even then, they weren't entirely sure it was her. Just Mark speculating.

Ben was sitting at the table pouring over the Jasper Killings. Abbi seemed to think there was a connection somehow to it. She'd marked pages here and there and he would go over them with a fine-toothed comb. Nothing stood out to him. Sure, there were a couple of similarities, but that could be all coincidence.

Wait a minute...

Abbi dragged a box into the room. Standing up, she sent a glance at Ben. He was engrossed in the book.

"You want something to drink?" she asked, looking at him on her way to the fridge. He was frowning.

Slowly he got up and walked towards her, the book in his hands. "Say Abbi. What did you mean by this part?" He asked turning to gaze at her, as he cradled the book in his hands.

That look would never get old to her. His green eyes sparkling with curiosity, his brow furrowed. His lips.... *my goodness he looks hot!*

She took the book from him and looked to where he pointed. She read the part twice, each time it didn't register. All she could think of was jumping him.

Good Lord Abbi... get a grip!

It'd been so long; she'd forgotten what pregnancy did to a woman's libido and she rather liked it.

"Um..." She looked up at him and bit her lip. "I ah. I'm not sure honestly."

He raised a brow at her and sighed. "Really?" He asked in amazement. "You wrote it? How can you not be sure?"

"It was a long time ago. I don't remember." She lied.

He sighed, scratching his head. "Right... okay." He motioned to the box she'd left in the middle of the room. "So... what's in the box?"

"That would be Christmas decorations. I thought we could put them up," She smiled.

Grinning, he pulled her into his arms, bringing her up tight against him. "Yeah? What about a tree, is it in there too?"

She linked her hands behind his neck. She leaned close, her mouth inches from his. Slowly she shook her head. "We have to cut one down."

Abbi heard the quick intake of his breath as she brushed her lips against his, felt his arousal against her.

Moonlit Road

Ben's lips caressed along her jaw, slowly he made his way to her ear as he ground his hips into hers and murmured, "When did you want to do it?"

She inwardly groaned. Abbi caught the innuendo.

She wanted nothing more than to strip him where he stood and jump his bones; but they were losing light. If she wanted to get the tree up and decorated before midnight, they had to get it now.

She pulled back and looked deeply into his eyes.

"Right now." she tugged his hand.

Ben eagerly followed her to the… *garage?*

"This is kinda kinky, and I love it, sweet one." His eyes sparkled when she turned the light on, a grin on his face. "But don't you think it's a bit cold out here?"

Instead of answering. She marched over to the peg board that held the tools on the wall and grabbed the axe.

Abbi passed it to him, looking up through her lashes, a soft smile on her lips, "I promise. I'll make it up to you… after the tree is in the house and it's decorated," she said.

He raised his brows and let out a low hiss, "You're a tease, you know that don't you?"

"I do, sorry. Now let's get going, were losing light," she laughed as he trailed after her, heading into the house to get their winter gear on.

They had been walking for a few minutes looking for the perfect tree. Abbi was chattering on, telling him what she wanted. One large enough that could be cut in half. Why she wouldn't just want two trees was beyond Ben. He didn't question her motives.

He was thinking back to the night he'd been alone in a forest just like this, nothing but trees and snow around for miles. The only thing keeping him sane was the woman that was now at his side.

He hadn't really thought much about it since that last night at the farm. But now, being here, he realized how easily he could have died that night. Good thing Smitty and Dean had found him when they did.

Neither of them knowing at the time that both were law enforcement. Dean was a convincing actor that was for sure.

Wait a minute... Ben stopped dead in his tracks. Walking with her head down, Abbi was concentrating on stepping in Ben's tracks in the deep snow as she pulled a sled behind, she didn't notice he'd stopped. With an "Oomph." She landed on her bottom, squarely on the sled.

Ben whipped around, "Oh my God Abbi are you alright?" he exclaimed worriedly. He bent down to give her hand up. "The baby? Is it okay?"

"As long as I'm not carrying her in my butt, I'm sure she's fine." Abbi laughed, taking his hand.

Tugging her to her feet, he looked taken aback. "Her? What makes you think it's a girl?" he asked placing a hand on her belly.

"Just a feeling. Don't worry, she could be a boy." she smiled.

"I just never really thought about the sex of it." He kissed her on the nose. "It doesn't matter to me what the baby is. As long as it's mother is healthy."

Abbi smiled. "Sweet talker." Grinning, she pointed and said, "There, that's the one."

He turned around, looking up to see a tree at least 15 feet tall. "Of course, it is." he said dryly.

Ben caught her as she threw her arms around his neck and planted the most sensual kiss on his lips he'd ever felt in his life. He was ready to take her on the snow right there when she handed him the axe. "Chop, chop." She winked and smiled as she smacked his ass.

"Woman," he growled, "you're doing this on purpose aren't you?" He grunted taking a swing at the tree.

"Of course!" Abbi giggled. "I need to get you all hot and bothered for later."

She walked around as he chopped at the tree. Looking for the perfect garland she'd said.

Which was perfect for him to think about Dean. It dawned on Ben before Abbi walked into him that maybe Dean wasn't who he said he was. Was he really a DEA agent like he claimed or was he like Gwendolyn, a washed-up actor now killer for hire?

And what was it that made Abbi think there was a connection to her book? That was still eluding him. He'd gone over every section she had marked off. Was he reading too much into it? Was the answer right there before his eyes? Maybe it had nothing to do with the book… but the movie?

He stopped for a second. He was starting to work up a sweat, he took his coat off and dropped it on the ground. *Wait a second...*

"Hey, you were there when Dean and Smitty came to the house, did you hear…?"

He turned in the direction she went off in. "Abbi?" Dropping the axe, he followed her tracks until he heard her crying. She was kneeling on the ground looking into the trees. He went down beside her and turned to see what was upsetting her so. Ben couldn't believe what he was seeing. There in the trees was the soft hazy glow of Franklin, with a woman at his side. Ben licked his lips, without taking his eyes off the sight before them he said, "Is that….?"

Abbi nodded, tears streaming down her face "Yes Ben, it's Hester." He pulled her into his arms as the apparitions disappeared into the trees.

"Please, don't cry Abbi, they're together at last." he soothed.

She clung to his sweater. "I know Ben. I wanted to bring her up here for Christmas. She was so lonely in that big ugly house. She had no one, not even a cat," she bawled.

"I know, love. Come on. I'm just about done chopping the tree." He pulled her up beside him and walked her back to the clearing.

"You're freezing. Why don't you go back to the house and I'll finish here?" he suggested.

She shook her head. "No, I'm fine. I'll wait." The temperature was dropping now; she could see her breath. She wasn't leaving him alone out here.

"Okay. At least throw my coat over you." He said. Picking it up off the ground, he shook the snow from it and draped it over her shoulders. She did put his coat on, not for herself, but to warm it for him. They still had a fair walk back to the house.

"One more hit Abbi and that'll be it." He grinned, picking up the axe. "Do I yell timber or something."

She chuckled, "If you like."

"Right!" He took one hard whack at it with the axe and with a yell any lumberjack would be proud, yelled "Timber!!"

He draped an arm around her shoulders. "How was that?" he murmured, nuzzling her neck. Leaning back, he looked at her for approval.

"It was perfect. You're perfect." she kissed him. Clinging to his lips she murmured, "Let's go home."

As they walked back to the house hand in hand, big fat snowflakes fell silently as the house came into view.

Ben looked at her as he pulled the tree into the garage. "Are you tired?"

"Surprisingly, no. Besides… we have unfinished business," she reminded him.

"Right! You get the stands, and I'll chop this baby in half." he rubbed his hands together in anticipation.

"Don't forget. We have to decorate them... tonight." she laughed.

He sighed, "I know, I know."

Tomorrow would be soon enough to figure out Deans role in all of this. Tonight, was for them...

Chapter 22

The living room looked like a Christmas card, a twinkling tree and a fire in the hearth.

Abbi sipped her hot chocolate as Ben put the last ornament on the tree in the living room; he had some skills she had to admit. He had done so well trimming the bottom half, that it looked like a full tree. The top half was already sitting on a table, decorated in their bedroom.

Taking her mug out of her hands he said, "So what do you think?" He sat on the couch and pulled her onto his lap.

"It looks fantastic," she shivered.

"Love are you still cold?" he asked noticing her red nose as he rubbed his hand down her arm.

She got up to throw another log on the fire. "A little, yeah."

She came back to his side and sat, laying her head against his arm. She turned her head to look at him. "Are you tired?"

Ben took her hand and linked their fingers.

"Are you?" He looked at her. He groaned when he saw her eyes filled with desire.

Abbi shook her head no. Wordlessly, she slowly climbed onto his thighs and settled herself on his lap. Ben thrust his hands in her hair, cupping her head, he brought her mouth to his in a crushing kiss.

She grabbed the hem of her shirt and tore it over her head. She needed to feel him against her bare skin. Her breast felt heavy and full straining against her bra for release.

Ben could feel her tugging on his shirt, as he ran his hands over her back; she felt like ice!

Tearing his mouth away, he grabbed her hands and searched her eyes, "Are you feeling alright?"

She tugged on his shirt again, trying desperately to rip it off him. "Of course. I'm fine." She mumbled in concentration.

"You're freezing, Abbi!" He took her by the hips and set her aside. Grabbing the throw off the arm of the couch, he wrapped it around her so only her head poked out. "Wait here. I'll be back for you."

Picking up her mug, she watched as he took off down the hall. Truth be told, she was incredibly tired. But that wasn't going to stop her from making love to him. She hoped…Her luck she'd fall asleep in the middle of it. This pregnancy was certainly kicking her in the ass. She couldn't remember being this tired or sick with the other two. *What do you expect Abbi? You're old enough to be a grandmother…True, I am, but clearly, I'm also young enough to be a mother again. Ha!*

Ben went back into the living room; he saw a smile tugging on her lips as she stared at the tree. She looked so beautiful sitting there in the soft lights. He wished he had the ability to read her mind.

Abbi looked at him. A grin played on his handsome face as he advanced towards her.

"No,no,no, " She chanted, squealing with laughter, she held her hands up to keep him back. "Don't you dare!" she laughed.

He didn't listen. He scooped her up in his arms despite her protest. Abbi had no choice but to wrap her arms around his neck.

"Not over my shoulder love. I'll carry you proper," he said, taking care to treat her as the fragile angel that she was he gently kissed her on the lips.

"It's bath time." he murmured against her mouth.

He could feel the thrilling shiver run through her body at his tone. He knew it would. Every. Single. Time.

How can I get so worked up over his voice for God's sake? It's not just the pregnancy either. Its him.

Abbi glanced around the dimly lit room. Candles flickered their soft glow, a hint of jasmine hung in the steamy air. Ben kissed her letting her legs go; she clung to him as her body slid along his hardness.

He deepened the kiss, while his hands worked the button of her jeans. Slowly he unzipped them sliding them down along with her panties over her hips.

She cried out when he took a step back. "Just a second." He murmured, taking his shirt off.

He gazed at her as she stood before him in only her bra. Removing his jeans, he kicked them out of the way. Reaching out, he hooked a finger into each shoulder strap, slowly he tugged them down her arms as he kissed her forehead.

Her breath quickened when his lips blazed a trail to her ear. His tongue flicked to that sensitive spot. *He will surely drive me mad* she thought as he dragged his mouth to her earlobe and bit it gently.

Abbi was no longer cold. As a matter of fact, she was on fire. She was so mesmerized by what he was doing with his mouth she didn't feel when he unsnapped the front of her bra. But there she was, standing, in all her glory, guiding his head to her breast.

She melted as he took one nipple into his mouth, while his fingers worked the other. She felt like ripping his hair out as his mouth lowered, again and again. He was kneeling before her now, his fingers trailed down her chest to her belly leaving a trail of goosebumps behind.

Ben laid a hand on the soft swell of her belly. His eyes stung with tears at the thought that his baby was nestled within. Ever so tenderly, he placed his lips there. He kissed her stomach and silently promised the baby within that they would be cherished just as their mother was.

His actions touched Abbi so, that she started to cry silent tears. She pulled Ben up to her, wrapping her arms around him. He took her thigh and hiked her up against his arousal.

She wrapped her leg around him, as he did the same to her other thigh. His hands splayed across her bottom, his mouth devoured hers, as he carried her to the waiting bath.

Just for this purpose, when they had built this bathroom, they had the hindsight to put it half sunken into the floor.

Not wanting to drop her, he set her down on the floor and held her hand while she gingerly stepped into the tub, sinking up to her neck. Abbi sighed in delight as the warm water lapped over her cold skin. But it didn't match the fire Ben had ignited within her. She wanted to reciprocate. She reached for his legs, as he stepped in the water before he could sit. She pulled him close to her.

He looked down at her, saw the mischievous grin, the glint in her eyes.

"Love…" he growled out as she touched him with her lips. She didn't do it often, and he never asked her to…but bloody hell he loved it when she did!

He just about lost it when her tongue ran along the tip of his cock. "Abbi…!" he hissed a warning. She needed to stop now if he was going to be of any use to her. As much as he loved her mouth on him, he loved being inside her more.

She leaned back, looking up at him innocently, she asked, "What?"

Ben lowered himself into the tub, sinking down, he pulled her into his arms.

His voice dripping with desire, he said smiling, "You know exactly 'what', you little vixen."

"You have room to talk." She yawned loudly.

"Am I boring you that much?" he laughed.

"Not at all. I'm just thinking, if you want to finish what we started, we should be heading into the bedroom. Otherwise I might pass out after and drown."

He sat there a moment, squinting in thought. Suddenly, he nodded and said, "Right. Let's go." Pulling her hand as he stood up.

Abbi laughed hysterically at his eagerness as they ran naked and wet to their adjoining bedroom.

She collapsed onto the foot of the bed, her legs hanging over the edge. Expecting any second for him to join her.

Where the hell did, he go?

She was too lazy to move, instead she called, "Ben?"

In answer she felt his hand on her leg.

Huh?

She looked down the length of her body. There he was kneeling on the floor, a wicked grin on his face.

"Oh my…" She was in for it now.

She shivered as his lips touched her ankle, trailing up to her knee and then her thigh. She wrapped her leg around his shoulders, urging him forward.

He was mere inches from her heat. It was pure torture waiting for his mouth to descend to her most private core. She cried out as his lips, moved to her other leg, trailing down to her ankle. She felt like grabbing fistfuls of his hair and yanking him to her. Mashing his face into…

Good Lord where did that come from? It was so unladylike. *I can't possibly do that…can I?*

Hell yes, she could! She pulled his head towards her. Whimpering she pleaded with him, "Ben… please!"

His throaty laugh was hot against her skin as his tongue flicked out to taste her. A soft moan escaped past her lips as she wrapped her legs around his head. That was all the encouragement he needed. He teased and suckled with his tongue as she writhed beneath him. If she squeezed her legs any tighter, he feared his head would pop. But still, he pleasured her, drank from her like she was the elixir for his soul. Now that he thought about is, she really was. She was his life.

Abbi couldn't take it any longer, she needed him inside her. Now! Pulling him up she wrapped her legs around his waist. Slowly, he eased into her. Reveling at how her warmth encompassed him. He could feel the tremors from within, telling him she'd already climaxed, and she was going to again; very soon.

Ben slowly withdrew, taking his time. He loved watching the emotions play over her face.

Abbi thrust her hips up to meet him a rhythm they had perfected long ago. She knew he was close, as was she. She also knew he was worried about going too deep. He really needn't be afraid. She stopped.

A panicked frown flashed across his face as he gazed into her eyes. "Love what is it? Did I hurt you?"

"Not at all." She flipped onto her stomach, brought her knees up under and backed towards him.

"We can't Abbi!" he cried, appalled.

Looking at him over her shoulder she said, "Trust me… we can, and we are. Come on, you'll see." She kissed him and felt him melt beneath her touch.

Bending forward she brought him with her. Hesitantly, he entered her softness once again. He so desperately wanted to stop, to tell her he wasn't doing it this way…but he couldn't. Gently he pushed onward through her silken folds until he was buried deep within her.

She purred as he swelled inside her. And moaned when he moved, matching her stroke for stroke… they both screamed in a frenzy of pleasure before collapsing into a quivering heap.

Chapter 23

Ben brushed his lips across Abbi's brow as he slowly eased his arm out from under her. It was morning and she was still sound asleep. He silently got dressed, watching her the whole time making sure she stayed that way. He had some business to take care of that she didn't need to know about.

Opening the door, he was greeted by all three dogs, looking expectantly at him; Molly was gearing up to bark her excitement at seeing him. Quickly he closed the door, taking care not to bang it shut. With a soft thud, he took her collar in his hand.

"Shhh girl." He guided her down the hall. "Come on guys. Let's get you outside," He said to the three as they trotted on his heels to the back door.

It had snowed overnight he noticed, Abbi and his tracks completely covered from last night. He watched as Brutus and Molly raced to the edge of the frozen lake. Looking down, he opened the door to let Lucy back in. Ben picked her up and dried her paws off, glancing out the window to check on the others as he did so, when something caught his eye. He frowned. *Our tracks are covered…than who are those?*

Just then his phone started ringing. Taking it out of his pocket, he saw it was Mark. Juggling Lucy and his phone he answered it with a quick, "Yeah?"

"Thank God your up." Mark said, alarm in his voice.

"Yeah, what's wrong?" Ben frowned, setting Lucy on the floor.

"You need to get over here man, like right now. Kim is having a fit. She's freaking out," Mark lowered his voice to a hushed whisper, "She thinks that one of the cops is a spy."

Huh... clearly, I'm not the only one who thinks it.

"I'll be right over," Ben said hanging up. He called the dogs in, quickly fed them and the cats and put his coat and boots on. Leaving a note for Abbi he headed out the door.

The sun was blinding off the new fallen snow when Ben stepped out the door. Twenty feet from the house he stopped and glanced down at the single set of footprints. It was hard to judge from the size of them if they were a man or a woman's, whoever it was, they had no business on his land. He followed them to Mark's yard, where they suddenly disappeared into the brush.

Mark was right, Kim was freaking out. He could hear her shouting clear across the yard. Making his way up the steps, he stopped as the door flung open.

Quickly he ducked, as two suitcases were tossed out, just narrowly missing his head. "Bloody hell Kim!" he shouted.

"Will you get the hell in here now." Kim hissed and ushered him inside as her eyes darted around the yard.

Ben raised his brows. "What is wrong with you?!"

"Me?!" Kim huffed. "There is nothing wrong with me. Now get the hell in here before they pick you off."

Ben shook his head in disbelief as he crossed the threshold. He jumped when she slammed the door shut and sent her a brooding look.

Ben glanced around the room as he shucked his winter gear. Ava and Noah were sitting at the table. Mark was leaning against the breakfast counter. Dean and Smitty were nowhere in sight.

"Thanks for coming man." Mark grabbed a mug, "Do you want a coffee?"

"Ah sure." Ben nodded. Looking at Kim, he took a seat at the counter, "What's going on with Dean and Smitty?"

Shrugging she said, "Oh, nothing much. Just that one or both are spies," she spat, as she cleared off the counter.

Mark sat the mug beside Ben, "See man I told you," he muttered out the side of his mouth as he poured the coffee.

Nodding his thanks to Mark, he asked Kim, "What makes you say that?"

"Cuz she's nuts." Ava mumbled, as she scanned the contents of the Jasper Killings.

Kim shot her a sour look. Turning her attention back to Ben she said, "Well, for starters they sneak around, watching constantly."

She jerked a thumb at the table, "Noah said the other day, Dean was rooting around in the garbage looking for evidence." She nodded self-satisfied. Finally, someone was listening to her.

Ben squinted and looked at her. "What makes you think it was evidence?" He folded his arms across his chest. "I mean, maybe he dropped something in there and was looking for it?" Ben raised his brows and leaned over, looking around Kim to Noah at the table. Noah silently mouthed his agreement. Ben nodded and straightened to look back at Kim.

Kim was scowling at him. "Yeah…? Yes, well maybe he didn't. Maybe he's in cahoots with whoever shot Brutus. I mean, just this morning I saw him over at your place. Peering in the windows."

Stonily Ben looked at her. "What?" He blinked. "What time was this?"

Kim visibly gulped. When Ben looked at her like that or anyone else for that matter, it meant trouble. Abbi would kill her if he did something to Dean.

"Ah… well, you know maybe it wasn't him." She squeaked.

"You know, it likely wasn't. My eyes aren't all that great." Turning to the table, she said, "Ava. Didn't I just say last week that I needed my eyes checked?"

Ava looked up from the book, "Nope."

Kim's eyes grew large as she gritted her teeth and made a fist at Ava. Spinning on her heel she looked back at Ben. "It might have been a..." She stammered, her mind racing... "moose! Yeah, now that I think of..."

"Kiiiim..." Ben ground out the warning.

Damn it! She hated when he used that tone on her.

"Okay!" She cried, wringing her hands. "Yes, it was him. He was scurrying around like a rat in search of crumbs, the sneak." She marched up to Ben and stuck her index finger in his face. "If you do anything to him... I'll.... Abbi will kill me." She stepped back, as he stood up, towering over her.

Ben weighed her words in contemplation.

She was right, Abbi would kill them both. Nodding in agreement he said, "Alright. What time did this happen Kim?"

"Fine!!" she finally gave in. "It was early. The moon was still out, but I could clearly see that it was him. Plus, I went and looked to see if he was on the couch... he wasn't."

What the hell was Dean doing that early in the morning? Was it before or after Abbi and me...?

"Does anyone know what time it started snowing," Ben glanced around the room, he added, "And when it stopped?"

"It started around 11:00 I think," Noah said.

"I got up around 3:00 and it wasn't snowing then." Mark said. "Why, what are you thinking?"

Ben was about to answer when they heard stomping feet on the porch. Someone was coming in. He stalked to the door and yanked it open. His breath froze in his chest. There stood Abbi, looking like the proverbial snow queen.

"Holy crap!" Abbi exclaimed, jumping. She caught the worried look on Ben's face just before it was replaced with a grin and a glimmer in his eyes.

Something was wrong.

"Morning love." He dropped a hurried kiss on her mouth, took her by the hand, and quickly pulled her into the house, and slammed the door shut behind her.

"Hey guys," She said taking her coat off she hung it on the coat rack. She rubbed her hands together, "What's up?" She asked, looking from one guilty face to the other.

Kim giggled nervously, shifting her eyes about. "What makes you think something is up?" She asked, nonchalantly as she leaned against the counter.

Mark poured her a cup of coffee and slid a plate of cookies on the counter.

Abbi grabbed a cookie and munched on it. Looking at Kim she said, "Because you all look like I interrupted something."

"Oh, for cripes sake." Ava said shoving her chair back as she stood up.

Ben shot her a warning look.

"What?! She has a right to know! Mom, Kim thinks Dean or Smitty is a spy for some mastermind, that's out to get you or Ben."

Abbi turned to look at Ben. "How long were you planning on not telling me this time?"

Ben gazed at her. She could read his so well. Guilt, shame, and fear stared back at her. But there was something more. A fire was burning in him. One of pure hatred. It wasn't for her, she knew. But something else.

He cleared his throat, taking her hand he said, "Abbi, you're not to get involved with this…" When she went to interrupt, he said, "I mean it. This isn't your fight. I've had my suspicions about Dean for some time now. Back at the farm…" Ben thought back to his first meeting with him. He had a feeling Dean wouldn't have hesitated to put a bullet in his brain given the chance.

He sighed, "Anyway. It doesn't matter; I'll take care of it."

"Ben, you're not alone in this." Noah said. "I think I speak for both me and Mark when I say this. We have your back man."

"What!" Mark barked in shock. Recovering quickly, he said, "Oh, ah. Yeah sure thing." He sent his newfound friend a wink and added, "Noah. I'll be right behind you buddy."

"Well now that's settled," Kim smacked her hands, grinning she asked, "when are you two planning the wedding?"

"Right now, Kim," Ben said. "You ladies get a head start. Us three, have a little business to take care of."

Abbi couldn't take her eyes off him as Kim and Ava steered her into the living room. She was terrified of what he was going to do, she just wished she could stop him…

Chapter 24

Abbi tried to pay attention to Ava and Kim as they tossed ideas around about the wedding, but her eyes were constantly drawn to the windows. The guys had bundled up and were out there, looking for what, she wasn't sure; *Dean and Smitty* she presumed. There was no way both men were spies. Too many officers had known them back at the farm. No. Dean didn't act like a police officer, but that didn't mean he wasn't.

Abbi got up slowly, not paying any heed to their chattering. Something was out there across the lake. After living in this house for years and looking out those very windows everyday she knew when something was out of place. She turned and went to the old china cabinet and opened the lower doors. The binoculars she'd left there when she moved, were gone.

"Guys, where did the stuff go that was in here?" she pointed to the cabinet.

"What are you looking for Mom?"

"My binoculars... I left them when I moved in with Ben." Abbi went to the windows again. Good, whatever it was it hadn't moved.

"Oh, hang on, I'll go grab them."

"What is it Abbi?" Kim came to stand beside her, worry evident in her voice.

"There's something across the lake." Abbi pointed. "See it?"

"Huh...I do. What is it?"

Moonlit Road

"I can't make it out, but It almost looks like a tent maybe."

"Here mom." Ava handed her the case.

Abbi quickly removed them from the case and looked through them. It was a tent alright and smoke... and a person.

Abbi saw Gwendolyn Pearce looking across the lake, directly in the direction of Ben, Noah and Mark.

"That bitch!" Abbi hissed.

"Who?! Let me see!" Kim said, grabbing at the binoculars. Abbi passed them to her on her way to the door. Grabbing her coat, and a set of keys she took off out the door, with Kim hot on her heels.

"Where the hell are you going?!" Kim yelled from the porch. "Sonofabitch she's going after her. Ava get out here. Now!!"

Abbi ran to the cars. She had no idea which vehicle the keys were for. Hitting the unlock button on the key fob, Marks truck honked in response. She hit the remote start. The engine came to life with a throaty rumble. Yanking the door open she jumped up into the seat as Kim and Ava hopped in. Sticking the key in the ignition, she threw the gearshift into reverse. She fully intended on backing out, but the truck had other ideas... it stalled.

Looking down in confusion, she saw there were three pedals.

Abbi cried, "What the hell is this?!"

"It's a stick Abbi." Kim muttered.

"I know it's a stick, Kim!" she shot back. "What's it doing in this truck!"

"Here, push that pedal in and hold it down. No. Not that one! The one on the left." Abbi did what she was told. "Now start it. I'll shift." Once again, the engine came to life. Kim grabbed the shifter, grinding the gears.

"You know... we could just take my jeep." Ava held up her keys, shaking them.

Popping his head up, Mark whispered, "Was that my truck?" as he laid next to Ben and Noah.

"Not likely mate…"

"Shush…" Mark said straining to listen.

The three of them were currently laying on their stomachs in the snow. Watching Dean and Smitty arguing over something down by the lake.

"Nah man. Seriously, I don't hear a thing." Ben mumbled, stretching his neck. God it was killing him lying in this position. He rolled onto his back and took his cell from his pocket.

"It is my truck!!" Mark hissed. Jumping up, he turned and took off towards the house as if he were in a race for his life.

"Why do you suppose his truck is running?" Noah asked glancing over at Ben who was frowning at his phone.

Ten missed calls?! Abbi! God the baby! Without a word, Ben scrambled up in a flurry of snow and took off after Mark.

Noah shrugged, turning back to the two down by the lake. Something was going to happen; he could just about taste it.

Ben came running up, taking in the scene before him, his eyes scanned the area until they found Abbi. She was sitting in the driver's seat of Marks truck, no worse for wear.

"Get out of my truck Abbi!" Mark yelled, his eyes bulging, as he stood in front of it; his hands spread wide on the hood, intent on stopping it if the need arose.

Ben walked to the side of the truck and opened the driver's door. "What are you doing love?" He asked, reaching in to turn the truck off before Mark had a conniption.

Moonlit Road

He passed the keys behind his shoulder, knowing full well Mark would snatch them up.

"Give me them! Don't you ever do that again, Abbi!" Mark's voice cracked as if he were about to cry. "I could hear the gears grinding down by the lake." he spat.

Abbi pushed Ben out of the way. "Come on, Ava," she called over her shoulder as she climbed down from the truck.

"Abbi! Where are you going?" Ben asked, grabbing her hand.

"She won't tell us. She took off out the door. Lucky for Mark she can't drive a stick." Kim said laughing.

Abbi stopped and turned abruptly. "I'm going after Gwendolyn, Ben. And you're not stopping me." she said.

Many times, he'd backed down when Abbi put her mind to something. This wasn't going to be one of those times.

"Where is she?" he looked at her, with the same amount of stubbornness. She stood there looking at him. He grabbed her by the arms. "Abbi. Where the hell is, she?!" He shouted. Instantly regretting it. He saw the hurt in her eyes, the sting of not what he said but how he said it.

He dropped his hands. "Love. I'm sorry." He shoved his hands in his hair. "But I can't allow you to go on some wild goose chase." He knew they had agreed not to tell anyone about the pregnancy just yet, but he didn't care. The woman he loved, who carried his baby was about to do something drastic and he was damned if he'd just stand there and not say something.

Taking a deep breath, he looked her deeply in her eyes. "If you're not going to think about your own life, then at least think of our baby's."

Abbi stiffened; her eyes blazed with a fire from within.

Oh shit… I shouldn't have said that.

"What did you just say?" Abbi asked in a steely voice.

"OH MY GOD!" Kim yelled, hopping around to Abbi's side. "You're pregnant?!?" She asked grabbing her by the arms. "I knew something was up!" she beamed, pulling Abbi into her arms.

"What?!" Ava paled, "I'm going to have a little sister. How?"

Mark had recovered quickly from his ordeal, "Do you really need to ask that Ava? Congratulations, man," He smacked Ben on the back. "Abbi, sweets." Mark turned on the charm, taking Abbi's hand in his, he kissed the back of it. "You're glowing already."

Abbi squinted at him. *Was he nuts?*

Ben needed to do some back pedaling and quick.

"That's not a glow Mark. She's pissed at me." Ben supplied.

"Oh. Well. Glad it's you and not me." Mark muttered as he walked away, he put an arm around Kim and Ava and said, "Ladies. Let's go into the house shall we and have a celebratory drink?"

Stopping in her tracks Ava walked up to Abbi. "Mom, are you okay?" Ava asked.

Oh, my dear sweet girl. Always concerned for me. Abbi shot her a watery smile and pulled her into her arms. Hugging her she said, "Yes baby girl, I'm fine. Go with the others. I need to talk to Ben." Abbi watched her walk away and into the house before she turned eyes on Ben. She could not believe he broke their agreement. She figured he'd have a hard time keeping it quite but to blurt it out like that was something she wouldn't forget.

"Abbi…"

Trying desperately to swallow the tears that stung her throat. She held up a hand. "Don't. Please." she whispered. "I can't lose you. Don't you understand that Ben?"

He looked down at the ground. Glancing up, he pointed to his chest and said, "What makes you think *I* can lose you? You think all I worry about is the baby?" When she was about to interrupt,

Moonlit Road

he said, "No. Don't deny it. I see it in your eyes! Abbi, I would go mad if I lost you. Why can't you understand that?" he asked vehemently.

She didn't say a word, she just stood there with tears silently rolling down her cheeks. He wanted to take her in his arms and soothe the hurt away, but she had to make that call, not him.

"Given the chance Gwendolyn wouldn't hesitate to shoot you again. And I'm sorry I broke our agreement. I shouldn't have mentioned the baby, not in front of everyone like that."

He couldn't help himself. He brushed a stray hair from her eyes. "I never told you this, but you were the only reason I never did anything back there in Tennessee. I knew if I had, I would have been killed." He leaned his forehead against hers. "I couldn't bear the thought of never seeing you again. Touching you again. Never being able to tell you I loved you one more time."

Abbi knew it wasn't just the baby he was thinking of. She knew the strength it took him to not do anything at the farm. He never was the type of person to stand down. She threw her arms around him. God, she loved this man more than life itself. Try as she might she could never stay angry at him. She leaned back, searching his eyes and laid her hand on his face.

"I love you more than anything in this world... but don't you ever yell at me again. Got it?" she said quietly.

"I'm sorry. I was desperate." He grinned. Sobering, he said, "I promise love. I'll never yell, shout or scream at you again for as long as I live. Truce?"

She smiled and nodded. "Yes, truce," She whispered against his lips.

Noah came running up to them as if the hounds of hell were in hot pursuit. Bending over he sucked in a deep breath. "Guys," he panted. "Call 911. Deans been shot."

"What? There were no gunshots. By whom?" Ben asked whipping out his cell phone. He tossed it to Abbi.

It had to be Gwendolyn…

"Silencer…Smitty. He just took off across the lake on foot."

Chapter 25

"Smitty?" Ben looked at Noah shocked. "Why would Smitty shoot Dean?"

"I don't know man; I just know what I saw. And that was Smitty holding a gun on Dean. Shot him right where he stood." Noah said shaking his head in disbelief.

"Did you call 911?" Noah looked at Abbi.

"Yeah," she nodded.

"Good." He replied, pulling out his own cell, he put it to his ear. "Both of you get in the house and stay away from the windows."

"We can't just leave Dean there to die." Abbi said. "We have to try and help him."

Ben steered her towards the house. "Go. Tell the others. I'll go with Noah and grab him." Abbi nodded, watching them walk away. Knowing if she didn't leave at that moment, she never would. Turning to go into the house, she stopped, glancing back at him. "Ben? I love you."

He stopped and looked at her. The look on her face said it all.

Silently he held his arms wide open. That was all the encouragement she needed. She ran to him. Throwing herself in his arms. She kissed his neck softly and said, "Please come back to me."

"I will Abbi." he brushed his lips against hers. He blinked at the sting of tears, "I love you too." He cleared his throat, "Now go, get in the house where it's safe, please."

He stood there until she was inside. He looked at Noah, and nodded, "I'm ready."

They stayed along the cover of the tree line at the edge of the lake. Noah held up a hand, signalling Ben to stop. Both men scanned the frozen surface. Smitty must have made it across. There was no open water that would indicate he'd fallen through. "What's across the lake?" Noah asked.

"Ah, nothing really. Just trees and brush." Ben said as he looked across. "Huh…There is something there I see. Looks like a tent or something."

"Come on. Let's get Dean and get out of here." They cautiously made their way to Deans side, darting between the trees for cover. He didn't look too good, but he was breathing. And awake. And mad as hell.

"That fucking asshole shot me in the goddamn leg! Help me up will you." he seethed.

"Not such a nice feeling being helpless now is it?" Ben asked, grinning at him. Which immediately was replaced with a scowl as he and Noah hoisted him up. "Ah, mind telling me why the hell were you snooping around my house this morning?"

"Yeah. Don't even say it. This is my karma." Dean groaned as they guided him back to the tree line. "And I wasn't snooping. I was watching Smitty looking through your windows." He motioned to the spot where he'd been laying not a minute before. "The bastard shot me when I asked about it."

"Sit on the ground a minute Dean," Noah said as he unzipped his coat. "Do you think it was left behind by someone. The tent that is? Like, who the hell would sleep in a tent in this weather?" Noah asked. Taking his belt off, he squatted beside Dean and wrapped it around his leg, tightening it as a makeshift tourniquet.

Ben pursed his lips. "It's possible I guess, or it could be a hunter." His hot breath, turning into a misty fog. "Whoever it is, they're trespassing. After what happened with Raven, Abbi bought the land up." Together, Ben and Noah lifted Dean up by the arms. Each man took a side, supporting his weight as they made their way across the yard.

Noah and Dean looked at Ben in confusion, Dean asked, "What the hell happened with a bird?"

Ben chuckled as they made their way up the back steps. "Raven Black is a man, not a bird." Ben jerked his head to the corner of the porch, "Get that chair will you Noah?"

Noah grabbed the chair, and together he and Noah sat Dean in it. "He's an actor that was pissed that I got the role in the Jasper Killings…. Wait a minute. You and Abbi went to school, together right?" he looked at Noah.

"Yeah. From kindergarten right up until she quit." Noah frowned, "Why?"

"Then you know who Raven is… He went to school with you two. His name was Roland Eddy."

"Roland Eddy, hell yeah I remember him." Noah chuckled.

Ben turned the door handle, it was locked. Odd.

"Right. Well he caused a plethora of shit a few months back. Almost succeeded in killing me and tried to win Abbi over. I beat the hell out of him. Thought I would end up in jail with him but luckily that didn't happen." Ben sighed, "If it wasn't for him being locked up, I'd suspect he was behind all of this."

Noah's eyes widen in thought. "Hell, Ben I remember that now. It was all through the police departments province wide…"

Ben raised his hand to pound on the glass; Noah's words stopped him from following through.

Dean interrupted; his eyes shut to the pain he was feeling. "Yeah man. States side too. He made bail just before, and I quote

Moonlit Road

every news source out there, 'Hollywood's most sought actor, Ben Everett's plane crashed'."

Something clicked in Ben's brain at Dean's words.

"Sonofabitch!" he muttered. "No wonder I couldn't shake the feeling back at the farm that everything was so familiar. My God! It was right before my eyes the whole bloody time." he tossed a hand towards Dean. "I thought it was you!"

"What? Me? What are you talking about?" Dean asked.

Noah was peering in the windows. "Uh, guys… why isn't anyone answering the door?"

Ben looked too. Something was wrong. Four people in the house and not one of them was watching out for them? He was sure they all would have been glued to the windows.

He cupped his hands around his face to get a better look, past the living room into the kitchen.

A feeling of dread came over Ben. His family was in there and something was terribly wrong. Then he saw it… "Someone is laying on the floor."

"What? Who?" Dean asked.

Ben stood there shaking his head. "I don't know. But I'm going to find out." He walked over to the planter in the corner of the porch. Lifting it up he took a key from underneath.

Heading back towards Noah and Dean, he flew down the steps and crossed the yard to the garden shed. Damn it, the lock was still on it. Taking a rock from the garden he smashed at the lock until it fell to the ground in pieces.

"What is he doing?" Noah asked.

"Hell, if I know." Dean said folding his arms across his chest as the two watched Ben make his way back to the porch.

"What're you doing with that axe Ben?" Noah asked.

Ben looked at him. With deadly determination he made his way to the French doors off Abbi's old bedroom. Noah helped Dean hobble along as they followed him.

Silently, Ben fitted the key into the lock. When he heard the click, he looked back at them both. "I'm going to put it in Raven's back if he's touched Abbi."

Dean and Noah looked at each other, slowly they looked at Ben as if he'd gone mad.

Dean scratched his beard. "Raven? Ah, buddy, what makes you think he's even here?"

"Oh, he's here all right," Ben mumbled and jerked his chin towards Dean, "He's the one that shot you."

Dean grabbed him by the arm. "How do you know?"

"Because. Everyone called me by my stage name, Ben Everett, including you, back at the farm. Only two people called me by my given name Ben Quinn. And the reason for that is because they already knew who I was."

Noah let out a low whistle, "...Daisy and Smitty."

"Right," Ben agreed.

"Hold up," Dean said.

Ben turned around, looking at him questioningly. "Now what?"

Dean and Noah looked to one another and nodded. Simultaneously they removed their pistols from their holsters and unlocked the safety. Dean gave a quick jerk of his head. "Okay. Let's go."

Ben slowly pushed the door open. Soundlessly they made their way into the house.

Chapter 26

In the dining area, Abbi was sitting on the floor with Kim and Ava. Ava was softly crying as Smitty stalked back and forth in the kitchen with a hand to his temple, the other held a gun.

She glared at Gwendolyn who stood guard by the front door. How Abbi wished she had a knife to stab in that heartless bitch's foot. The foot that had just kicked her in the stomach. She laid her hand over the spot, praying it hadn't hurt the baby.

"What are you going to do with him?" Gwendolyn asked motioning a hand toward Mark's still form. Blood pooled from the gash on his head onto the floor; caused by the butt of Smitty's gun.

Smitty stopped and cast a deadly look in her direction. He wanted to put a bullet between her eyes for kicking Abbi the way she did. Resisting the urge to raise his gun, he shoved his hands into his hair. "Will you just shut up and let me think a minute," he screamed.

He hadn't meant to hit Mark, he thought it was Ben coming in from the living room. That prick. Taking his Abbi away from him. He had planned on doing much worse to him when he got his hands on him. But when he'd seen it was Mark who fell to the ground. He didn't know what to do. His plans were all shot to hell.

Smitty's face was itching him like crazy. Rubbing his jawline, he paced back and forth like a caged animal.

The plane crash was the perfect idea. But oh no, Ben Quinn was not an easy kill.

You should have learned that from the last time... the voice said to him.

No. I should have killed him in the States. But no... Tennessee has the death penalty. It had to be done here. It would never do to be dead; I'd never get to be with Abbi then.

Kim looked at Smitty. She was watching him since he'd thrust his hands in his hair. She blinked in amazement when she watched as it slid sideways.

What the hell?! He's wearing a wig! She couldn't help but to stare. Waiting for the minute that it slipped clear off his head.

"What the hell are you looking at?" Smitty sneered, "You want to say something to me?" he yelled out, spitting at her.

It was on the tip of Kim's tongue to say a madman when she felt Abbi shift against her. Silently conveying to her to keep her mouth shut. She turned her gaze towards the darkened hallway. Seeing the shadow of a man, she silently prayed whoever it was, had a gun.

"Yeah. I didn't think so," Smitty cackled.

Abbi looked at him, stalking the room like a crazed man, picking at his jaw. Her eyes widened as she saw his face crumbling where he was picking it. She froze as he stopped and looked directly at her, taking deliberate steps towards where she sat on the floor.

Desperately, she inched back against the chair behind her. Squeezing her eyes shut, she turned her face away as he reached out to touch her hair. Instead he dropped his hand and held it out to her.

"Abbi, come with me." Smitty said.

Immediately she was transported back in time a few months. When she'd had the BBQ in this very back yard. She heard that voice before. It was Raven's. She snapped open her eyes to him.

"No…" She slowly shook her head. "It can't be… you're in jail."

"Oh." Smitty, said. A smug smile on his lips, "I can assure you it is."

Abbi watched in horror as he touched his jaw and worked an edge loose, pulling it upward.

Dread immediately washed over Abbi as inch by inch the lifting of a silicon mask, revealed the face of Raven.

He held out his hand once again, "Abbi?" When she didn't move quick enough to his liking, he pointed his pistol at Kim's head. "Now. Shall we?"

A wave of heat hit Abbi full force. Taking s deep calming breath, she slowly nodded placing her hand in his.

"You bastard!" Gwendolyn spat out. "It was you! You're the client Sheriff Martin was talking about. You're the man in charge. It was never him. You never intended on paying me for organizing the takedown of that plane!" She accused Raven.

Raven spun around; his gun leveled at Gwendolyn's chest. "You're right. I never did have any intention. Do you think I could honestly pay you on the agreed upon amount?" He threw his head back and cackled. Raven looked at Abbi accusingly, "I would have, if Ben never got the part in your movie. But that's okay, I'll take care of him later."

The bile rose in her throat as the pain in her stomach increased. Placing her hand on her belly she desperately tried to swallow it back down, but it was no use. The projectile vomit hit Raven squarely in the face, momentarily blinding him.

Kim kicked out as Raven took a step back. He landed flat on his back, gagging and wiping frantically at his face.

With pure rage Raven jumped up, gun raised, he pointed it squarely at Abbi's chest.

"Not so fast asshole," Dean yelled, aiming his gun at Raven.

Noah was next, holding his gun on Gwendolyn.

"Raven you need to put that gun down right now!" Dean advised him, threateningly.

Never lowering his arm, Raven glanced at Dean and Noah. "Well how do you like that Abbi? Your man is nowhere in sight. Doesn't even have the guts to come and save you." He sneered. "I'll tell you what I'm going to do," he said to the room at large, jerking his gun in Abbi's direction.

"I'm going to shoot her. And then… you two will shoot me. You see it's the perfect plan." He turned desperate eyes to Abbi. "We'll always be together this way Abbi." he said in an insane whisper.

"Like hell you will," Came an ominous voice from the darkened hall.

Raven spun towards the voice. Fear replaced the maniacal expression on his face as he saw an axe making it's spiraling way towards him. Shock registered in his eyes as the head buried itself deep in his chest. The last thing he saw before hitting the floor was a dark and self-satisfying look on Ben's face.

Dean hobbled over to Mark, reaching down he checked for a pulse. "He's breathing." he called out, as sirens could be heard wailing in the distance.

Ben glanced at Abbi, rushing to her side, he caught her just before she hit the floor. "Love are you okay?" his worried eyes searching her face.

She gripped his shirt as a wave of dizziness hit her again. "Yeah. "I'm just having a lot of pains," she panted.

Ava stalked over to Gwendolyn, pulled back her arm and sucker punched her in the side of the face, knocking her to the floor. "You ever kick my mother again I'll cut you."

"She kicked you?" Ben looked down at Abbi's ashen face. "Where?"

"Her stomach." Kim looked at him, a grave expression on her face, "I'll call Doc."

Moonlit Road

Ben grabbed a chair, pulling it away from the table he said, "Here sweet one, sit," as he guided her on it.

He looked over to where Noah was, still holding his gun on Gwendolyn. Dean was sitting on the floor next to Mark, who was conscious now, pressing a towel against the gash on his head.

Ben was seething mad. Without thinking he walked up to Gwendolyn and wrapped his hands around her neck.

She grappled at his hands as they squeezed tighter. Her eyes protruding out of their sockets.

"Sonofabitch Ben!" Noah dropped his gun to the floor with a clatter as he tried pulling Ben off Gwendolyn. "Ava give me a hand!" He shouted.

Ava jumped on Ben's back, pummeling it futilely. Abbi saw what he was doing. Despite wanting to do the same thing to the woman, she couldn't let him have that on his conscience too. Raven's death would be bad enough.

"Your baby needs its father, Ben," she said.

Ben turned at the sound of her voice. Tears filled his eyes when he saw her arms wrapped around her middle. He dropped his hands and went to her. Sinking to his knees, he wrapped his arms around her, and softly placed his lips against her belly. Abbi ran her hands through his hair as she bent forward, she laid her head against his back. "And so, do I," she cried softly against him, as the pain once again wracked her body, her tears soaking his shirt.

Abbi couldn't hear what he was whispering against her stomach, but she knew his pain.

Please God… Don't let me lose them both…

Chapter 27

"Something didn't feel right back on the farm." Ben said as he felt the reassuring squeeze of Abbi's hand in his. He glanced at her. She was sitting beside him, silently conveying to him her love, giving him the strength to continue.

With everything that had happened since that fateful day; three days ago, when Raven decided to hold his family hostage. This was the first chance the police had of hearing his side of the story. Cops, detectives and agents from both sides of the border, were there to listen gather information from all parties involved. They held Ben's fate in their hands.

He was thankful for Dave aka Dean. Despite the man's arrogant ways, he'd turned out to be a stand-up man. He'd insisted helping Noah to convince their fellow officers to hold off on questioning Ben, until Abbi and he found out their baby was thriving.

Gently squeezing her hand back, he looked at the men in blue gathered around their dining room table.

One detective asked, his pen hovering over a notepad, "When did you discover there was something off?"

"I can't pinpoint when, just an overall feeling of foreboding." Ben thought a moment. Leaning forward he said, "And the fact that Smitty and Gwendolyn seemed to really know each other." Ben looked at Dave, "Just the way they talked about the plane crash, you know? Saying how lucky I was they were so close by." He frowned. "Plus she took her mask off in front of him as if it was an everyday thing. I didn't realize until the other day that she really didn't know who he was either."

"And you didn't put the puzzle together until when?" A detective hedged.

"I had my suspicions. But it was when Raven shot him." Ben jerked his head to the man on his right, one that he now considered a friend. "Dean...er... Dave, I mean, had mentioned about the plane crash and used my stage name. That's when it occurred to me through the whole ordeal, only Raven and Gwendolyn called me by my given name. To be honest. I thought it was Dave that was somehow in on it."

"Well thanks for the vote of confidence there, bud." Dave shot him a sly smile.

An FBI agent cleared his throat. "With all due respect, Dave, you are a bit of an asshole."

The chief investigator spoke up. "I think that pretty much clears up any unanswered questions." He paused. Looking directly at Ben he said, "This is against protocol in situations like this. But due to your status and everything that has transpired in the last few months I think we can come to a decision in what direction we will take. If you and Abbi will excuse us for a moment, we will let you know shortly."

Ben saw the look on Abbi's face as they left the room in silence. She was terrified. He guided her into the living room where everyone was waiting. Ava rushed over to them as they entered the room and tearfully hugged Ben. "I'm so sorry you're having to deal with this." she muttered, pulling away. "Mom." she hugged Abbi, "It's all going to work out."

"I know baby girl." Abbi hugged her back tightly, tears streaming down her eyes. *It has to work out....* She couldn't even begin to think what life would be like with Ben in a jail cell serving time for the death of Raven.

"So now what?" Mark asked, holding his head. He was currently sporting a bandage wrapped around it. He'd got off lucky with a dozen stitches and a concussion.

Moonlit Road

Ben took a deep breath. "We wait." he said.

Making his way to the window, he watched as big fluffy snowflakes made their way softly to the ground.

He wondered, if the police did decide to arrest him, how long would it be before he could look out this window again. To look into Abbi's eyes again. *Days, months, years...?* His worried thoughts were interrupted with a car pulling in the driveway, followed by another... Abbi's SUV. Luke and Lane had arrived. He watched as his parents exited the first car followed by her sons and another man he'd never met before.

Ben turned to look at Abbi. She was sitting near him in the chair by the fireplace. Looking so... forlorn. He gently touched her shoulder and said, "Love? Get the door, will you?"

He saw the instant puzzlement cross her lovely face. Grinning, he took her hand and said, "Trust me." Together they walked to the door. She opened it and squealed at the sight of everyone standing there. Holding her arms wide, she embraced both her sons, as Ben's parents did the same to him.

A cough had everyone looking at the man that stood there alone.

Why does he look so familiar...? Abbi frowned, desperately searching her memory.

"Oh, my goodness!!!" Abbi cried in delight as she held her arms out to him, welcoming him with a big hug.

"Abbi it's so good to see you again!" He laughed as he held her at arm's length. "I see you're going to have a little one. When are you due?" He beamed, looking down at the slight swell of her belly.

"Yes!" She let him go, and put an arm around Ben and smiled, saying, "Mid May is when I'm due. Will you excuse me for a moment?"

She rushed to the living room. She had some quick explaining to do, "Hey Mark. How are you feeling?"

"Not too bad sweets." He gave her a sideways look. "Why do you ask?" She sat beside him, talking in hushed tones she explained what was going on.

"Like I said I'm sorry, I completely forgot I'd asked Lane to bring him up when they came for Christmas. He was all alone though, and he did help me…"

Mark waved a hand at her. "I get it, I get it!" He rubbed the stubble on his chin. "So, he knew me… but not Ben?"

Abbi nodded her head vigorously, grinning. "That's what he said."

She watched as he leaned back and took a deep lungful of air. As proud as a peacock he said, "Well, what're you waiting for? Bring him in." he grinned.

Smiling Abbi left his side and returned to the foyer, where only the man stood. "Where did everyone go? Never mind. Come with me," she grabbed his arm and hurriedly steered him to the living room where Mark stood waiting.

"Mark, I'd like you to meet the cab driver who took me to the airport that night. Leo…" She looked to him realizing she had no idea what his last name was.

"Markell." He supplied standing there with his hat in his hand grinning.

"Leo my man! What a coincidence, we have the same name. Mark, Markell… yeah. You know what I mean," Mark laughed as he came forward with his hand outstretched. "So, I hear you didn't know who Ben was?" He chuckled.

Abbi watched as Mark turned on the charm offering Leo a seat. She grinned knowing that she'd had a hand in making at least one person's wish come true.

The smile on her face stayed as she felt Ben come up behind her. Putting his arms around her, he laid his hands on her stomach. Softly he laid his lips against her neck. "Love, they are calling me back in the room now." Her smile faltered as she swallowed the lump that sprang to her throat and silently nodded.

Moonlit Road

Turning within his embrace, she looked up and gazed into his eyes. Laying her hand on his cheek, she whispered, "I love you so much. Whatever happens I'll wait for you."

He laid his forehead against hers and covered her hand with his. "I love you too sweet one." He softly kissed her on the lips, memorizing the feel of her mouth beneath his, clinging to her sweet taste. Wishing that he could stay in this moment forever.

"Ben." Noah cleared his throat. "They need to get on with this, the snow is picking up and they all have to get back to the city before the storm sets in."

Nodding, Ben backed away. Holding onto Abbi's hand he turned and followed Noah into the dining room. Pulling a chair out for her to sit he took the one next to her and sat down.

"Ben." The lead investigator began. "After careful consideration of the evidence at hand and all that has transpired in the past few months it is our opinion that charges against you in the death of Raven Black will…" The man stopped and looked at his fellow agents and officers. All nodded as one. The chief nodded back.

Abbi looked down to where her and Ben's hands were clasped in her lap. *Please God don't let them take him away from me,* she silently pleaded, as she squeezed his hand tight. So tight, his fingers were turning white from lack of blood flow. The suspense was killing them both.

Ben knew by the grip Abbi had on his hand that she would have a meltdown if the decision wasn't favorable. Hell, he was on the verge of one himself. Reaching over, he gently lifted her chin. Searching her eyes, he silently conveyed to her how much he loved her with just one look.

Clearing his throat for attention, the lead investigator said, "We all believe the death of Raven Black was indeed self-defence. Given the fact that you have two police officers to back your statement."

A cheer went up from the back of the room. Ben and Abbi turned as one, to look at their family and friends standing there.

Moonlit Road

Ben nodded his thanks at Noah, who nodded in return. He then looked at Dave who shot him a quick wink. Smiling, he turned back around to face the men before him.

"Not so fast." Banging the table for order as if he were a judge beating his gavel, the investigator continued when all fell silent.

"You possibly will need to go to court. Considering what Raven Black has done to you and Abbi in the past, I'll be talking to the crown attorney, and I'm confident you will never need to step inside of a courtroom."

"As for the attack on Gwendolyn Pearce. It is felt by all of us that your actions were justified. Given the fact of everything she had done to both you and Abbi and that of your unborn child. And yes, even your dog. She, however, will face the consequences of her actions and will be charged for all offenses she has committed, which is quite lengthy. Any and all charges against you, will not be filed for now. Until I speak to the Crown, stay in the country and you're free to do whatever you please." The investigator stood up, looked at his fellow officers and said. "Let's get the hell out of here. We have a long trip home."

ೞೞ

It had been a week since the investigators had come and gone. The house was silent as Ben and Abbi laid in each other's arms. Their house guests had long since retired to their rooms, all caught up in the excitement of Christmas Eve.

She snuggled up to him, laying her head on his chest. Listening to the steady beat of his heart as he absently drew his fingers over her bare skin.

He was watching the news on the TV. The reporter came on with breaking headline news. Abbi turned and sat up watching as scenes from the plane crash played across the screen. Remembering that day that felt like yesterday, she couldn't help

Moonlit Road

the tears that slipped down her cheeks. Ben sat up beside her and put his arm around and pulled her close to his side.

"It has been confirmed that Ben Everett leading actor of the Jasper Killings and soon to be released movie, Stoned River has been found alive and well." The male announcer said.

"Took them long enough." Ben snickered, looking at Abbi.

"Shush," she responded, covering his lips with her hand.

"Coincidentally, it was found that the actor's plane had been purposely shot down. Investigators linked it to Raven Black, the same actor, who not more than a few months ago made headline news by getting bail" The announcer looked to his co-anchor *"Get this... after an attempted murder on Ben Everett. Raven Black was found dead by a self-inflicted gunshot wound in his home."*

Abbi turned to Ben and sent him a dumbfounded look, "Wha...," she started to say. He placed his finger on her lips, hushing *her* this time.

"Wow! What a crazy mixed up world we live in." The female announcer added.

"That's not even the half of it. Ben Everett is thee most sought-after actor in Hollywood... and... he just announced his retirement...."

Ben clicked the remote, shutting the TV off as he laid a soft kiss in the palm of Abbi's hand, the one that still covered his mouth. He laid back and pulled her on top of him.

She gestured to the TV, "What was that all about," she asked.

"I forgot to mention to you that Simon Smith, you remember the lead investigator…?" He looked at her with his brows raised. At her nod, Ben continued, "Yeah. Anyway, he called earlier this morning and told me he'd talked to the Crown. They are not going forward with any charges against me and there will be no court proceedings. That's the reason for the story of Raven *shooting himself.*" He looked in her eyes, watching and waiting for a reaction.

"What're you thinking love?" He asked, brushing the hair out of her eyes.

She sighed. "I'm thinking… That I am the luckiest woman in the world right about now." She smiled looking down at him.

He raised a brow. "Oh yeah?" a quick devilish smile flitted on his lips.

"Mhm. I got my Christmas wish." She smiled, as she kissed his chest. Feeling his heartbeat quicken at her touch, she slowly made her way up to his lips. Clinging to his mouth, she was so utterly moved by this man. When he reached up and grabbed her by the arms, she let out a squeal of laughter as he flipped her onto her back.

They both grinned at one another as he sat back and straddled her legs.

Abbi looked at him. Watched as his face took on a serious note.

"What is it?" She asked, her smile wavering.

"Back there, on the farm. I thought I would never see you again. If anything had happened to me, I'd have died never knowing that I was going to be a father… I thank God every day for bringing you into my life Abbi Petersen."

"Ben," She sat up, tears stinging her eyes. She gazed deeply into his, seeing the love shine there for her.

"Abbi. You are the love of my life, the mother of my child. And I can't wait for the day that you become my wife." He took her face in his hands. Kissing her with a fiery hunger as he laid her back on the bed.

He turned her insides to mush. She sighed contentedly as he nuzzled her neck and giggled uncontrollably when he growled "Woman you drive me insane," next to her ear.

She silently thanked God and the Universe for bringing this man home to her.

All that she'd wanted for Christmas, and for the rest of her days was right here in her arms…

The End

Dear Readers, thank you for taking the time to read Abbi and Ben's story.

Stay tuned for more exciting adventures from the Pearl Lake series ~ Tina Marie

Manufactured by Amazon.ca
Bolton, ON